***"Go away and don't come here again."***

"I will not," she said, kneeling and planting her fists on her hips. "If you want solitude, go find it somewhere else."

"Don't try to bully me," she added. "I'm not easily intimidated."

"Liar," he mocked. "You're shaking inside your little designer swimsuit. You'd be yelling for help if your mind weren't spinning with terror."

"It'll take more than wishful thinking on your part to prove that."

His sweeping glance took in everything, from her discreetly lacquered toenails to the dull glint of gold at her wrist and ears. His smile radiated scorn. "How much more?" he asked softly as he unbuttoned the waist of his denim cutoffs.

***CATHERINE SPENCER*** suggests she turned to romance-fiction writing to keep from meddling in the love lives of her five daughters and two sons. The idea was that she would keep herself busy manipulating the characters instead. This, she says, has made everyone happy. In addition to writing novels, Catherine Spencer also plays the piano, collects antiques and grows tropical shrubs at her home in Vancouver, B.C., Canada.

## *Books by Catherine Spencer*

HARLEQUIN PRESENTS PLUS

1623—DEAR MISS JONES

HARLEQUIN PRESENTS

1406—THE LOVING TOUCH
1587—NATURALLY LOVING

HARLEQUIN ROMANCE

3136—WINTER ROSES

# CATHERINE SPENCER

# *Elegant Barbarian*

*Harlequin Books*

TORONTO • NEW YORK • LONDON
AMSTERDAM • PARIS • SYDNEY • HAMBURG
STOCKHOLM • ATHENS • TOKYO • MILAN
MADRID • WARSAW • BUDAPEST • AUCKLAND

ISBN 0-373-11682-9

ELEGANT BARBARIAN



This edition published by arrangement with Harlequin Enterprises B. V.



**Printed in U.S.A.**

# CHAPTER ONE

SOMEONE was watching. Not from behind, where sea gulls wheeled and screamed under a cloudless sky and the surf dragged at the sand, but from somewhere along the bluff.

Laura lifted her head a fraction and saw him at once. He stood atop the cliff, legs straddling the earth while his gaze swept the landscape with the easy possession of a Viking warlord surveying his spoils. Until it fell on her, and then it froze.

There was a world of hostility in his stance, in the absolute stillness of his tall, bronzed figure against the bright summer sky. He was warrior and hunter, and she both enemy and prey. Instinct rather than conscious thought had her easing the straps of her swimsuit back on to her shoulders, and reaching defensively for her towel. A chill that was completely at odds with the weather raced over her skin. For the first time that she could remember, the cove became a place of fear, its solitude a threat.

Without deigning to watch his step, he began the long descent to the sand, his legs moving with a smooth, determined rhythm that paid no heed to the tussocks of grass or the outcroppings of rock that had tripped many another careless visitor. His shadow loomed closer, sliding across the beach toward her.

Laura knew a powerful urge to run, quickly, before he was close enough to touch her. Pride held her captive. He was the interloper, not she.

He came to a stop no more than a yard from where she waited. He was a tall man, powerfully muscled, with hair bleached almost white by the sun. His skin glowed but his eyes remained cool, their color measured less by their blue intensity than by the reserve and blatant aggression in his vivid gaze.

"Where have you come from?" He imbued the question with a threat so soft it was deadly.

It never occurred to her not to answer. She indicated the big stone house on the cliff at the far end of the cove. "Up there."

"I don't like company," he said, with that same chilling calm. "Go away and don't come down here again."

She didn't know why she didn't just do as he asked. She hated scenes and had never been one to encourage confrontations if there was any way to avoid them. But the unwarranted contempt in his glare goaded her into defiance. "I will not," she said, kneeling and planting her fists on her hips. "If you want solitude, go find it somewhere else."

He flexed long fingers in implicit threat. Gathering courage where she could find it, Laura decided that, despite their callused strength, he had the hands of an aristocrat, not an assailant. "And don't try to bully me," she added. "I'm not easily intimidated."

"Liar," he mocked. "You're shaking inside your little designer swimsuit. You'd be yelling for help if your mind weren't spinning with terror."

She eased into a sitting position and smoothed sand from the edge of her towel. "It'll take more than wishful thinking on your part to prove that."

His sweeping glance took in everything, from her discreetly lacquered toenails to the dull glint of gold at her wrist and ears. He contemplated her well-cut hair, her Italian leather sandals that sat precisely parallel to each other, and finally brought his gaze to bear on her knees now held primly together by her tightly clasped hands. His smile radiated scorn. "How much more?" he asked softly, and tore open the snap closure at the waist of his denim cutoffs.

A blush raced up her neck to flood her face. He wouldn't dare! Would he?

The rasp of a zip told her he would, and the formidable common sense that was her trademark urged her to make a dash for safety. It wasn't out of reach, by any means—two hundred yards at the most to the foot of the steps that led up to the house and help in the shape of Frank, her great-grandmother's gardener.

But something held her back. Perversity? Or an insane, delicious curiosity?

Mesmerized, she stared at his feet planted in front of her on the sand. Long, elegantly formed, deeply tanned, just like his hands. Who was he?

She'd almost drummed up the nerve to open her mouth and ask, when the cutoffs slid down his legs, obscuring his ankles. She let out a yelp of horror. Involuntarily, her eyes flew up, past the flaring muscles of his calves and thighs.

His laughter taunted her. "Go back to your mommy, little city girl," he jeered, his teeth a dazzle of white, his eyes twin fires of satanic amusement. "Don't you know it's dangerous to talk to strange men?"

Lazily, he stooped to retrieve the cutoffs and tossed them on to a convenient slab of rock. Stepping over her as if she were of no more account than a sand flea, he sauntered down to where the surf creamed and tumbled up the beach. Without hesitation, he waded into the chilly water until it was deep enough to slap at his black swimming trunks then, with expert timing, he curved himself forward and speared through the green wall of an oncoming wave.

"I met a man on the beach this morning," Laura told her great-grandmother at lunch. She frowned at the plate of oysters on the half shell set before her and hoped she didn't sound as discombobulated as she felt. Honey Bee was eighty-nine, but her faculties were as sharp as a woman half her age.

Across the table, Honey Bee dabbed with her napkin at a spot of sauce on her chin. "Someone from the Haida village?"

An image of bright blue eyes and blond hair flashed across Laura's mind. "No," she replied quickly.

Too quickly. Honey Bee looked up, her glance shrewd. "What makes you so sure, my love?"

He'd been tall and muscular enough to pass for one of the native Indians from whom Frank often bought fish, but, "He wasn't dark enough," she said, "and he was . . . unfriendly."

Honey Bee shrugged. "I haven't heard of any strangers in the area, but then, I don't get out as often as I used to. He's probably an artist, or one of those kayakers who wash up on shore every once in a while. He'll probably be gone by tomorrow."

A kayaker? But of course! That would explain his tough, weathered look. She'd been so busy not staring at what she feared he was willing to display that she hadn't even thought to look for the means by which he'd arrived; but a kayak could well have lain hidden among the rocks, and it was the only explanation that made any sense.

There was nothing to see from Carter's Cove but great swells of ocean that ran all the way up the Sound from Japan to crash on the headlands at each end of the bay, and nothing to find except the oysters and clams that lived along the fringes of the beach. The only land route into the area was the private lane that ran a full three miles from Honey Bee's house to the road that wound out from the fishing village of Pearce. As a tourist spot, Carter's Cove offered little, which was precisely why Laura escaped to it as often as time permitted. No doubt Honey Bee was right; by tomorrow, Laura would have the entire bay to herself again.

Honey Bee was wrong. He was there again the next morning, digging clams down by the water's edge. At the sight of him bent over, all bronzed muscle and tousled blond hair, Laura's heart gave a little jump. It was because she was annoyed, she told herself, and would have ignored him had he not beaten her to it by glancing up and turning an indifferent back at the sight of her.

"I thought you'd be gone by now," she said, marching straight up to him.

"Dream on," he drawled, scooping a handful of Little Necks into his pail. "I'm here for the duration."

"And how long will that be?"

"Until *I* decide I'm tired of the place, which means no time soon."

"You realize, of course, that you're trespassing?"

He paused from his digging to lean on the handle of the clam fork. "Save your breath," he sneered.

"Private property ends at the high-water mark and, even if it didn't, it'd take more than your say-so to move me on. Go lose yourself."

"Has anyone ever told you that you're a very rude man?" she observed.

His grin was shockingly attractive. "Not only that, but I curse a lot, and take advantage of women. Better run and hide, sweet face."

The man was barbaric! "I should have known better than to try to exchange a few civil words with someone like you," she snapped. "You ought to be kept in a cage."

His hands shot out to lock bruisingly around her wrists. With dismaying ease, he yanked her almost off her feet and hauled her up close. A week ago, if someone had told her she was going to find herself alone on a deserted beach with the angriest man she'd ever met, she'd have known exactly how she would react: with extreme caution and a healthy dose of fear!

She would have scorned the suggestion that such an experience would cause her blood to swirl with excitement. It must be terror that had her trembling, and brain fever that made her look at his mouth and wonder what it would feel like on hers, because he was no more her type than she was the kind of woman given to such wild, absurd imaginings.

His eyes narrowed, fringed by sultry lashes the color of smoke. "I ought to teach you a lesson," he whispered savagely, his breath skimming her face with the familiarity of a lover, "so that you learn to keep that tongue of yours on a leash."

"Let go of me at once!"

He did, and she almost buckled at the knees. Flinging out one hand to maintain her balance, she grabbed at his arm. If his skin was warm and smooth as velvet, the underlying texture was pure granite.

His rage died as suddenly as it had arisen, leaving his eyes cold and watchful. Crazy as it seemed, it was as though her touching him, even fleetingly, was the most outrageous intrusion of privacy. She snatched her hand away and stifled the apology that almost spilled out of her mouth. He was the one guilty of social infractions, not she.

He recovered the clam fork and held it with the tines pointing at the sky. He reminded her of an oil painting entitled *Sea God* that she'd once hung in the gallery. He possessed the same ruthless aura of power, the same pagan indifference. Who was he? What was his past?

Stabbing the end of the clam-fork's handle into the sand, he dragged a trough between her feet and his, and extended it several yards toward the bluff. He didn't need to explain. She knew at once that he was staking out his territory.

"Keep to your own side," he advised her tersely, and swung away, supremely confident that she would honor the frontier. He had spoken!

Well, it happened to suit her just fine. She'd have preferred to have the cove to herself, but he'd been right when he'd said he wasn't trespassing. Honey Bee's property didn't extend the full width of the beach, nor did it include a water lease. That being so, Laura was willing to settle for joint tenancy. Such a hostile neighbor wasn't likely to intrude on her peace, nor she on his.

She spread out her towel and propped up her little canvas beach chair. Setting her sandals neatly side by side, she smoothed sunscreen lotion on her arms and legs. Then, satisfied, she plopped a wide straw hat on her head and settled down with her book.

It was the middle of July, and a whole blissful six weeks of summer stretched ahead with nothing to interrupt them. Only Archie, her partner, knew where to find her and, even though they had a major art show slated for October, she didn't expect to hear from him. With any luck, she wouldn't have to be back in the city until after the Labor Day weekend.

Between the pages of her novel, which rated number one on the *New York Times* bestseller list, a man stared across a room at a woman, his dark, mysterious eyes filled with hunger. Down at the water's edge, the stranger sifted through the sand with long, easy strokes that had the sun kissing the muscles of his shoulders and caressing the graceful length of his spine each time he stooped to collect the tiny gems that would grace his dinner table. And through it all, his eyes remained on his task, except for an occasional glance out to sea.

It was hot. Perspiration slicked her forehead and the smooth skin behind her knees. Rose would not approve. "Men perspire," she'd instructed the teenage Laura, on one of the few occasions that they'd spent the summer together at Carter's Cove, "and horses sweat. Ladies glow dewily—if they must."

If truth be known, Laura couldn't care less. She'd stopped trying to win Rose's approval about the same time that she'd decided she never wanted to be like her. But by whatever name one chose to call it, the sticky, prickling heat on her skin was uncomfortable, and distracting. It was hard to persevere with Chapter

Four of the bestseller when the cool surf invited, not more than twenty yards away.

The sand burned the tender skin of her feet and had her hopping like a jackrabbit to cover the distance between her towel and the ocean. Contrarily, when she reached the water, the waves that rode halfway up her calves held the sting of icy northern currents. Shock had her gasping for breath and retreating. But, like a playful child, the surf chased her and sprayed her thighs.

*He* snickered, and stopped digging to lean on the fork and watch the show. Slewing her gaze away, she prayed for fortitude, tugged the straps of her ivory maillot firmly into place, and followed the only option pride allowed her.

The waves closed over her, banishing the memory of summer's heat. Rising up beyond the line of breaking surf, she fought for breath and began a dogged breaststroke, pumping her arms and legs before the blood in her veins stopped flowing altogether. Six strokes out, six back, then a dignified rush through the shallows to the blessed warmth she'd so carelessly abandoned.

His grin outshone the sun but held nothing of its kindness. The denim cutoffs lay beside the clam pail. The black swimming trunks clung to him, seeking to anchor themselves to something more yielding than his trim hips and finding not an ounce of spare flesh anywhere. How did they resist the tug of the surf? she wondered, staring fascinated as he sauntered toward the onrushing waves.

He disappeared into their embrace and was gone so long that she almost began to worry. Then his head emerged, dark as buckwheat honey, and he began a strong, lazy crawl as though to advertise that he was impervious to the cold and had all the energy and time in the world to enjoy himself.

"I hope you wind up in Japan," she muttered, and, sprinting back to her towel, flung herself facedown on it. Gradually, her limbs thawed and her heart slowed. Pillowing her head on her hands, she closed her eyes and let the sun dry her. It was too lovely a day to waste on animosity.

"You're baking, sweet face."

If there'd been the slightest hint of concern in his words, she might have forgiven him for dragging her back from that pleasant half world of sleep where dreams were punctuated by the real cries of the gulls. But his voice was laced with an irritation that she knew was mirrored on his face, even though, when she lifted her head to glare at him, the sun shone straight into her eyes and all she could discern was the haloed outline of him.

"So?" she asked coldly.

He shrugged those wonderful shoulders and turned away. "So nothing. Fry, for all I care. I'm just warning you, that's all."

"Well, mind your own business. And stay off my half of the beach."

He spared her a scornful laugh that left her feeling as childish as she knew she sounded. "Sure thing," he said, and strolled back to his clam fork and pail. Hefting them both in one hand, he climbed the bluff with the same energy with which he swam: effortlessly, and with the graceful sort of coordination that marked a natural athlete.

She slept in the nude that night, because the soft cotton of her nightgown felt like sandpaper on her shoulders. When she looked in the mirror the next morning, the skin she'd so foolishly exposed to the sun glowed fiery red. She looked like a parboiled lobster.

"Laura!" Honey Bee was appalled. "That's a terrible burn, child. How did you happen to be so careless?"

It was his fault. "I fell asleep on the beach," she said, and winced as the straps of her bra cut into the tender flesh.

She spent the day in the shade of a wonderful old magnolia that her great-grandfather had planted for his bride right after he'd built the house. "I love this garden," Laura sighed, staring up through the interlacing branches to the brilliant sky. "I remember when I was little how I used to wish I could live here all year round."

"That wouldn't have suited Rose at all," Honey Bee said. "Three or four days was more than enough for her—and still is."

Laura felt a stab of mild irritation at the mention of her mother. "Why does she bother to visit at all, then?"

Honey Bee's smile was almost cynical. "Because she's afraid I'll cut her out of my will if she doesn't make a token effort to butter me up."

"Tell her you're planning to leave your money to an animal shelter," Laura suggested wickedly. "That'll spare her having to take time away from what's even more important to her—finding another husband."

"Speaking of which," Honey Bee said, her eyes lighting up with disgraceful pleasure at being handed such a perfect opening, "why isn't there some nice marriageable man in your life, my love?"

Laura smiled guilelessly. "Actually, I've got five nice marriageable men in my life, Grandmother—four already framed and hanging in the gallery, and another being shipped from Italy. Pity they've all been dead for more than three hundred years, isn't it?"

"You inherited your great-grandfather's dimples, as well as his audacity!" Honey Bee tried to look severe. "You're forsaking love and happiness for a career."

Goaded into forgetting her sunburn, Laura sat up too quickly and let out squeak of mixed indignation and pain. "I'm doing no such thing! I'm very happy and lead a perfectly full and wonderful life."

"Rubbish! How can your life be perfectly full and wonderful without Mr. Right?"

"Honey Bee!" Laura couldn't contain her amused exasperation. "The world is full of attractive men, but the right one for me won't conveniently fall out of the heavens on command, you know. If he shows up of his own accord, all well and good, but I don't have either the time or the inclination to go big-game hunting for him. In fact, right now I don't need him. I've got too many other things cooking."

"Every woman needs a Mr. Right," Honey Bee scoffed.

"If you really believe that, then why have you never married again? It hasn't been for lack of offers, I'm sure."

"Because no one could ever replace the man I had. Stephen has been dead nearly fifty years but he was the only one for me, Laura, and if I had it all to do over again I'd marry him in a flash, even knowing there'd be tears and heartache ahead and that I'd spend far more years a widow than a wife."

Despite all her claims to the contrary, Laura felt deprived for a moment. Deep down, she supposed she agreed with her great-grandmother's philosophy. A special man, a special love...was there a woman alive who didn't like to think they were in the cards for her, one day? But not now! Laura had trouble enough juggling all the other interesting happenings in her life without the complication of a serious love affair right now.

After dinner that evening, when the air was cooler, she decided to walk off some of her energy. The tide was high, leaving only a narrow strip of sand exposed, so she chose the route along the top of the bluff from which to admire the last of the sunset.

She was almost at the far side of the bay and ready to turn back the way she'd come when a faint gleam of light filtering through the trees on her right caught her eye. A few paces ahead of where she stopped, a cabin which had been abandoned for years sat in a cozy hollow surrounded by tall firs and cedars that sheltered it from winter storms. Without a second's hesitation, she changed direction and followed the trampled grass that was the path.

Someone had taken up residence. He'd even done laundry. It hung from a line stretched between one of the posts supporting the porch and a sapling fir. Tea towels and a couple of pillowcases kept company with underpants whose brevity made her blush. Next to them, a T-shirt that had seen better days shared clothes pegs with a pair of well-worn jeans that looked as soft as chamois.

At the other end of the porch, the same someone had rigged up a makeshift shower, the sort that campers and sailors often used, with a foot pump and a length of hose. A bar of soap, incongruously pink, sat in a chipped saucer and, next to it, a bottle of shampoo. Tatty old sneakers with no laces lay upside down on the railing, apparently drying out. Near by, a fishing line and tackle box were stacked against a wall, next to a clam fork and a pail that she'd seen before.

The worn boards under her feet sloped toward the outside. Whatever color they'd once been stained had long ago faded but they were still sturdy. She made not a sound in her soft-soled shoes as she crept toward the window.

Barefoot, he sat at a table, bent over a pile of books and papers littering its surface. The oil lamp that had caught her attention cast a yellow glow, gilding his hair to the color of ripe wheat. He wore a dark blue shirt, with sleeves rolled up to his elbows, and a pair of jeans rather more respectable than those hanging on the clothesline. He'd have looked the complete outdoorsman, thoroughly at home in his spare surroundings that lacked any sign of modern convenience, had it not been for the heavy manuals over which he pored and the gold-rimmed glasses he wore that lent him a rather scholarly air.

Suddenly, he pushed away from the table and stretched. She'd have had to be blind not to notice the spread of his shoulders, and a congenital liar not to admit to being rather dazzled by the sheer magnificence of him. It was fashionable for many of the men she met through business to spend their time in gymnasiums, pumping iron by the hour in order to develop a physique that this man obviously came by naturally. What a pity he was such a barbarian with it all.

Leaving his glasses on top of the books, he ambled toward a door at the rear of the room and disappeared. She supposed, from what she could see, that there must be a kitchen at the back, because the only other items in the front room were an old armchair covered by a woven Indian blanket, a camp cot on which lay a neatly rolled sleeping bag and a couple of pillows and, separating the two items of furniture, a small table holding a second oil lamp. A floor-to-ceiling stone fireplace covered the far wall, its hearth neatly swept.

It occurred to her then that, even though there was no fire, she could smell smoke. It wove around her in a delicate thread of flavor, subtly aromatic and reminiscent of childhood Christmases. She closed her eyes and inhaled, searching her memory.

Cuban tobacco, of course! Someone was smoking Havana cigars, the kind her uncle John used to enjoy after dinner on Christmas Day. But her uncle had been dead more than fifteen years, and Laura didn't believe in ghosts. Logically, the only person in the vicinity likely to be smoking was the stranger, and, since it was impossible for cigar smoke to pass through solid walls, she was forced to the disturbing conclusion that there was another exit from the cabin apart from the door to the porch.

Cautiously, she backed away, planning to retreat from the scene the same way she'd arrived—with undetected stealth. The indignity of being caught snooping with her nose glued to the cabin's window, and thereby subjecting herself to a fresh outburst of abuse from its tenant, held little appeal.

But her concern came too late. Cigar clamped between his teeth, the stranger leaned against the rain barrel at the bottom of the porch steps, watching her make a fool of herself.

## CHAPTER TWO

SHORT of vaulting over the railing into a patch of poison ivy, Laura had no choice but to confront him.

"That's a filthy habit," she announced, deciding that here was a classic case of attack being the best form of defense. "I once read that kissing a smoker is a bit like licking clean a dirty ashtray."

"If you're waiting for me to offer to let you prove the point, you're wasting your time," he drawled. "I'm not in a kissing mood."

His effrontery left her speechless.

"Close your mouth," he went on, climbing the steps toward her with a determination that made her heart race nervously. "You'll catch fewer flies that way—unless, of course, you were about to explain what the hell you're doing spying through my window."

"I saw the light," she said lamely, "and wondered what it was... then I saw your laundry."

"The sight of which got you so excited that you just couldn't resist peering through the window to see if I had a spare set of clothes!"

He was, without question, not only the rudest man she'd ever met, he was also the most conceited. "Actually," she retorted, "I found myself wondering why any man with half a brain would waste his money on expensive cigars when he'd be better off spending it on something that would be of benefit to him. Smoking is bad for your lungs and those——" she pointed a disdainful finger at the sneakers drying on the porch railing "—are a disgrace and probably bad for your feet."

He sank down against the post that supported the roof overhang and proceeded to make himself comfortable, slouching back on one elbow and extending his crossed legs until they stretched diagonally across and halfway down the steps. Holding the cigar between his thumb and forefinger, he blew a perfect smoke ring into the still air and watched it disintegrate before replying, "Don't lose sleep over it, since they happen to be my lungs and feet, not yours, and therefore none of your business."

"Fine." She cast about for another means of escape. The cabin stood at her back; on one side of the porch was the patch of poison ivy, on the other a makeshift tarpaulin cover for some sort of machinery. Her only exit lay over his semi-supine body and down the steps. "In that case, I'll save my breath, and if you'll move aside I'll be on my way and leave you to go to hell in a handcart."

He looked up at her from under his smoky lashes, a lazy grin on his face. "I don't feel disposed to move, sweet face."

"Then how do you expect me leave?"

He shrugged, and inspected the tip of his cigar. "You obviously pride yourself on being an intelligent woman. Figure it out for yourself."

The evenings were usually cool, once the sun had dipped behind the mountains on the western shore of the Sound. Normally, she'd have worn a pair of pants to go walking, there would have been no problem, and she'd by now be on her way. Tonight, though, out of deference to her sunburn, she'd chosen a wrap-around skirt of butter-soft cotton that didn't chafe her skin, and she wasn't about to give him an unobstructed view of her thighs as she clambered over him to freedom.

"You're no gentleman," she snapped, coming to a halt mere inches away from him, and staring pointedly at his out-thrust legs.

"And you're no lady," he replied, unfazed, "because if you were you'd find some other way to satisfy your frustrated appetites than by sneaking around and peering through a man's window."

It would have afforded her the utmost satisfaction to kick him, but about the same time that she lifted her foot to take aim he somehow read her mind. His hand shot out to snag her ankle in a remorseless grip. "Unwise," he murmured. "Very unwise, sweet face. You're mistakenly assuming my fetching smile and easy charm hide a forgiving heart."

"A cockroach has more charm, and I've seen alligators with more attractive grins!"

"What a beggar for punishment you're turning out to be. Now you're going to have to apologize twice."

"Apologize?" She choked back an incredulous laugh. "When hell freezes over!"

He shook his head. "I can see it's going to be a long night," he sighed. "Thank God you've got good legs!"

As if to test the veracity of his words, he ran his fingers appraisingly up her calf. The shock waves rolled all the way past her knees and made her thighs tremble. "You're a pig," she declared when she could manage to draw breath.

"Now is that fair? First a cockroach, then an alligator, and now a pig?" He touched the skin behind her knees, a fleeting kiss of his fingertips that was over before she could voice her outrage. "Have I resorted to calling you names, even though you are the one who trespassed on my privacy and spoiled the serenity of my evening?"

She'd never fainted in her life, but there was a first time for everything, and what other explanation could account for the dizziness that threatened to topple her right into his lap? She felt disconnected from her limbs, even though the heat that sapped her energy stemmed from his fingers tracing beguiling patterns down her calf. "I'm sorry," she managed, clutching the post beside her.

"And you will not intrude on my privacy again." He made it a declaration of certainty, not a request.

"I will not intrude on your privacy. Now will you please let me pass?"

"I suppose I must." He sighed with patently phony regret and indulged in a last exploration of her ankle. "What a pity. You have delicious skin, even though it is a bit overcooked at the moment. See what happens when you ignore my warnings?"

He was trying to embarrass her but what she hoped he didn't realize was that he was unnerving her, too. She liked to think of herself as sensible without being neurotic. In the city, she didn't leave her doors unlocked, nor did she invite disaster by frequenting lonely parks and dark alleys. Yet she found herself wishing there were a reason to remain in this isolated spot with this man whose name she did not know. Worse, she wanted him to go on touching her because, even though he was merely amusing himself at her expense, she found the experience exhilarating. The bald fact was that some streak of insanity she'd never suspected held her in thrall to the danger of him.

Fortunately, he grew tired of his little game. He swung aside his legs and waved his cigar in languid invitation for her to proceed.

What's your name? she wanted to ask. Where have you come from?

But he'd already dismissed her from his thoughts. Even before she'd gained the path leading back to the bluff, he was staring off into the distance, preoccupied with weightier concerns. His complete indifference to whether she ran or walked made her urgency to escape unscathed seem ridiculous and reduced it to what it really was: the ignominious departure of an uninvited and unwelcome guest.

Pride had her using her sunburn as an excuse to avoid the beach for the rest of that week, but the plain fact of the matter was that feminine curiosity had her itching to learn more about the stranger. For the first time in her life, she was shamefully tempted to chase a man down—go big-game hunting, as she'd so scornfully put it to her great-grandmother just a few days before.

Fortunately, before she succumbed to the urge to plant herself on the beach in the shade of a sun umbrella, in blatant invitation to anyone who might feel disposed to exchange the time of day and offer a few morsels of information about himself, the weather suddenly changed. A low-pressure front swept in from the Pacific, saving her from herself.

"How would you like a trip into town?" she asked Honey Bee instead the next afternoon when the rain showed no sign of abating. "I don't know about you, but I'm ready for a change of scene for an hour or two. We can stop by the store, if you like."

Honey Bee's face lit up. "That's a splendid idea, my love! I haven't been to Pearce in weeks and I don't remember the last time I had a good visit with Jessie. What a dear child you are to suggest it."

What a sneaky weasel she was to suggest it! Laura knew full well that Honey Bee and Jessie Morrison, owner of the general store, would exchange gossip the entire afternoon. Jessie was a mine of information; what wasn't to be learned by consulting her wasn't worth hearing in the first place. If anyone could provide information about the stranger, Jessie could be counted on to have the facts on file.

But Jessie was no one's fool. Laura knew she'd have to couch her queries discreetly if she didn't want it rumored about town that Honey Bee Carter's great-granddaughter was showing uncommon interest in a man no more suited to a woman like her than pigs were to flying.

Honey Bee unwittingly spared her the effort. "I know," she said, in answer to Jessie's surprised delight at seeing her, "it's been too long since I paid a visit, and I suppose it would have been even longer if Laura hadn't gone and got herself a miserable sunburn yesterday. Do you carry anything that'll help, Jessie?"

"Calamine lotion," Jessie decreed, searching the shelves behind the counter. "Makes you look a sight, but it's the only thing that works short of sitting in a tub full of water and baking soda. Here you are! I knew we had some, somewhere."

"What a pity you didn't have it on hand yesterday, Laura," Honey Bee said, "though I don't suppose it would have helped, unless you'd taken it down to the beach with you and your stranger happened to be there to dab it on your back."

"Stranger?" Jessie's nose fairly twitched with excitement. "You got strangers down in the cove, Honey Bee?"

"Just one," Honey Bee said. "A kayaker, we think. Not a local fellow, from the way Laura described him. Fair, you said, didn't you, my love?"

It was ludicrous that the image of deep blue eyes and wild blond hair should so vividly spring to mind, or that Laura should envision skin the warm rich color of teak, and a smile as cool as winter. It was unnatural for the flesh behind her knees to break out in minute tremors, as though his fingers were at that very moment trespassing past all bounds of gallantry or discretion.

"As far as I can remember," she said, pretending to examine the contents of the glass-topped freezer where Jessie kept ice cream jammed right next to fishing bait.

"Oh, you mean the hermit!" Jessie swooped on the information with glee. "Big man, right, Laura? Yellow hair that hasn't seen a barber's shears in Lord knows how long?"

Laura shrugged and managed to lie superbly. "I guess so. I can't say I paid that much attention."

"Bought supplies here a week or so ago, he did." Jessie pushed forward a chair for Honey Bee, then settled on her high stool behind the counter and prepared for a lengthy session of revelations. "Basics that would last a family of five a month or more. Paid cash, too. Didn't want to run up a tab like other visitors. Suited me, I can tell you. Didn't have much to say for himself, though I gave him opportunity enough. Barely civil, you might say. Didn't seem to appreciate the interest. Said he's looking for peace and quiet and don't welcome visitors. Not that anyone'd want to go calling, considering that cabin he's renting. Not fit for a dog, if you ask me."

"What cabin?" Honey Bee enquired.

"Why, that old fishing shack just the other side of the cove from your place. You know the one, Honey Bee. Belonged to Ned Kelly back before he won the lottery and went to live in the city. It's been standing empty ever since, as far as I know. Must be awful damp and dirty by now." Jessie let fly with a cackle of glee. "Reckon that hermit must feel right at home."

Laura's objection was out before she could contain it. "Oh, that's not fair! He's clean enough!"

"Is he now?" Jessie grinned slyly, showing all ten of her remaining teeth. "Reckon you took more notice than you're letting on, then, Laura. Got an eye for a good-looking man, even if he don't wear a three-piece suit and a silk tie. Reckon you're Rose's daughter, right enough!"

Rose had outlasted or outlived four husbands with undimmed energy and was currently searching for a fifth. Repelled by her mother's belief that any man was better than no man, Laura bitterly resented the suggestion that she was cut from the same cloth. Ignoring Jessie's remark, she turned to Honey Bee. "Grandmother, do you fancy fresh fish for dinner, if anyone on the boats is selling?"

"That would be lovely, my love."

"Then we should go and check now, if you still want to have time to stop by the library before it closes."

They arrived on the dock just as one of the shrimp boats came in and a fresh burst of rain swept down. By the time they arrived at the library, it was pouring.

Laura was shaking water from her umbrella when he appeared, a stack of heavy books wrapped in plastic under one arm. "Allow me, ma'am," he said, pushing open the door for Honey Bee. Then he noticed Laura and raised his brows in reluctant acknowledgement. "Oh, it's you again," he said ungraciously.

He wore a yellow windbreaker over jeans, and yellow sailing boots. His hair was plastered to his head and his eyes, bluer than ever as though to defy the gra afternoon, surveyed her dispassionately.

She nodded, aware that Honey Bee's birdlike gaze had fixed itself expectantly on her face. The sociably acceptable thing would have been to introduce him, but it was out of the question for any number of reasons, the most pressing being that Laura hadn't the faintest notion of his name.

When the silence threatened to grow awkward, Honey Bee took matters into her own hands. "I'm Beatrice Carter, young man," she announced, "and I don't believe I know you."

The smile he bent on her great-grandmother was so charming that Laura's insides quivered. "I'm Jackson Connery," he said.

"How do you do?" Honey Bee was in her element, sizing up the situation and arriving at all sorts of unwarranted conclusions, Laura was sure. "It appears that you've already met my great-granddaughter, Laura Mitchell."

"Yes," he said, and condescended to address Laura again. "I'm surprised to see you here."

"At the library?" she asked, hackles rising. "Why? Did you think I couldn't read?"

His brows curved reproachfully this time, and a hint of laughter warmed the cold intensity of his gaze. "I do tend to associate you with other places," he said ambiguously, "and other pursuits."

Lord, he might not be much of a clotheshorse, but he was handsome! Laura turned away and told herself that it was just annoyance that left her feeling so rosy. "This is the man Jessie mentioned, Grandmother," she announced and, in case he'd assumed her blushing gaze had been directed at him in admiration, added with uncommon malice, "You remember—the vagabond living in Ned Kelly's old cabin."

"Ah, yes." Honey Bee's gaze swung from Laura's face to his, and a smile played over her mouth. "As I recall, it's a very primitive little place. You must come up to the house for dinner, Mr. Connery, and spend an evening with us. We'd enjoy the company, and I'm sure you'd enjoy the change."

"I'm sure I would, too, Mrs. Carter——"

"But not tonight," Laura interrupted, urging Honey Bee through the door. "I didn't buy enough shrimp for three."

"Child!" Honey Bee exclaimed delightedly, as Laura let the door swing shut in Jackson Connery's face. "You were rude to that charming young man, and furthermore, you're blushing. Is there something you haven't told me?"

"Quite a bit," Laura said shortly. "For a start, he's one of the most impertinent men imaginable and anyone less disposed to be charming I've yet to meet."

"I see." Honey Bee's chuckle suggested that she saw a lot more than was good for her and that it had triggered her imagination into overdrive.

"I doubt that," Laura said repressively. "He's not our type, Grandmother, and I don't think it was very wise to encourage him to pay a visit. You know next to nothing about him, after all, and the little bit I've learned doesn't exactly recommend our getting to know him better."

"You were always a mannerly child," Honey Bee remarked with apparent irrelevance. "It's not like you to treat someone with the unkindness you showed Mr. Connery. Why does he disturb you so much, my love?"

"He looks the type to steal the family silver."

Honey Bee's laugh had everyone turning her way. "Oh, you do delight me," she crowed, "especially when you try so hard to deceive yourself."

Liar, he'd said, that first day on the beach. Your mind's spinning with terror.

It had been true then, and it was true now. To so many people she was Laura Mitchell, co-owner of the prestigious Sunderland Gallery, living proof that a woman no longer had to depend on "old money" and family connections to make a success of her life. But *he* delved past her public image to touch the private person underneath with an intimacy and perception that left her shaken.

"I'm not deceiving myself or anyone else," she told Honey Bee firmly. "You're letting your imagination get the better of you."

"It isn't my imagination that's put the bloom in your cheeks, my love," Honey Bee insisted. "It's that man over there who's pretending to search for a reference book but who's really trying to sneak a look at you."

Like a fool, Laura had to see for herself. Jackson Connery rewarded her with a disgruntled scowl and swung his back to her as though she was an affront to his existence.

She wished she could as easily dismiss him, and was both dismayed and puzzled to discover that, as far as he was concerned, "out of sight, out of mind" didn't seem to apply. It was as if her emotions were a compass needle suddenly gone wild and leading her badly astray.

She knew herself too well to think she could simply accept without question the unexpected curve destiny had thrown her way. She was a realist who liked answers that made sense—and Jackson Connery smacked too much of a romantic fantasy whose magnetic pull had to be defied and overcome. Was it that—the need to put her willpower to the test—that drove her back to the beach the next day, rather than the fact that the weather had turned sunny again?

He was bent over an old row boat, patching it with some sort of tar, and gave no sign of noticing her as she walked down to test the water. It was chillier than ever, thanks to the recent cool spell. Just in case he happened to look up, though, she didn't falter as she waded into the surf and struck out for the calmer water beyond the line of breakers. She wasn't about to fuel his need for entertainment a second time by dithering in the shallows and turning blue with cold. Once was enough.

If he kept his mind on it, he'd have the dinghy seaworthy in time to catch the tide, and could probably make it around the headland to the next cove and back before the afternoon was out. But she had to show up again, wearing that body-clinging swimsuit and, for all that he cursed under his breath, his attention kept swinging from the job at hand out to where she was bobbing about in the surf. Damned woman! Why couldn't she have found some other place to play sea nymph?

Of course, if truth be known, it wasn't all her fault even though she did seem to take delight in getting under his skin. Mostly, the problem was his. He couldn't ignore her; couldn't ignore himself, either, or the insane messages his body was sending to his mind, and that was what really infuriated him.

He should never have given in to the urge to shock her into flight that first morning. He still couldn't fathom where the impulse had come from but he did know, with an insight that later disgusted him, that for one wild millisecond of insanity, as his cutoffs had slid to the sand, he'd been paralyzed with a jolt of driving hunger as his mind had filled with images of how her slender, cream-smooth body would feel beneath his. Dangerous thoughts . . . dangerous woman.

They'd warned him this sort of thing could happen but he hadn't really believed them. You might find yourself obsessed with women, wanting to stare at them, even touch them, they'd warned. It's natural enough, but watch how you react if you don't want to wind up in trouble. You won't be given the same benefit of the doubt that other men might get. And don't try to bulldoze your way back into your old social circles. If people decide you don't fit in any more, all you'll get by insisting is a lot of grief you can do without.

He'd have found the advice amusing—if he hadn't forgotten how to laugh. He couldn't imagine wasting precious time on women or life in the fast lane when all he wanted was to be left alone to nurse his battered spirit. He didn't need anyone. He most assuredly did not need *her*, with all that sophistication overlying the naiveté of a baby. One look at the twenty-two-carat gold jewelry, the designer clothes, and the calm assurance that life owed her the very best it had to offer, told him how diametrically opposite they were to each other.

That silver-haired charmer of a great-grandmother, though, was different. Refined and delicate as a cameo, she nonetheless possessed a shrewdness altogether too acute for his peace of mind. She was the kind who saw too much—and he was the kind who found women like her irresistible. Funny how, despite everything, he still had a soft spot for old people.

It was enough to make him question how tough his resistance really would be if it came under serious fire. Until recently, the idea that it might let him down would have been almost as preposterous as his attraction to *her*. To Laura.

"Laura . . . Lorelei . . ." He spoke the words aloud, heard the alluring musical elegance of them fly away on the breeze, and looked over his shoulder to make sure no one had crept up behind and heard him making an ass of himself. He'd be better occupied nurturing the anger that had become second nature to him. It was his second-best defense, after indifference. Either people couldn't get close to him, or they didn't dare.

Against his will, his gaze swung out across the waves. What the hell was she trying to prove, staying out there this long? Did she think that if she ran the risk of dying from exposure he'd care enough to go in and save her? Fat chance! The only person he was interested in saving was himself.

When she emerged from the shallows, he was still engrossed in his task and appeared supremely indifferent to her presence. In fact, she was almost past him before his voice stopped her in her tracks. "Enjoy your swim?"

"Yes." Surprised, she turned back toward him, but his head was bent over his task as though she was of too little consequence to merit a direct glance. "It was wonderful."

If she hadn't known better, she'd have thought he was laughing inside. "Not too cold for you today?"

"Not at all," she said gamely, containing a shiver. "It was very refreshing. Bracing, you might say."

"Liar." He inspected his handiwork and slapped a last daub of tar in place.

"I beg your pardon?"

He bent lower, absorbed with feathering brushstrokes over the patch to create as smooth a finish as possible to the old wooden hull. "I said, you're lying. Again."

"That's what I thought you said," she replied frostily. "May I ask how you arrived at such a conclusion?"

"Because," he said, and there was no mistaking the laughter now, "your lips are blue and your teeth are chattering even faster than you are."

No doubt he was right, but, "What do you care?" she had to know.

It served her right for asking. The amusement vanished and he gave her such a careful once-over out of those incredible blue eyes that she wondered if he was actually counting her goose bumps.

At last, his gaze slid up to rest thoughtfully on her mouth. "I don't, sweet face," he said.

## CHAPTER THREE

NOT for a minute had Laura expected Jackson to take Honey Bee up on her invitation to dinner, but she was both surprised and dismayed when he stopped showing up at the beach. If it weren't totally absurd, she'd almost have believed she missed him. What was more likely, she decided, was that she missed their verbal skirmishes for the extra spice they'd added to the days.

She'd have liked to believe it was a return to unsettled weather that kept him away, except that she knew he was too hardy to be put off by something as inconsequential as a little rain and wind. Plagued by the thought that he might have decided Carter's Cove wasn't such a desirable spot after all, she took to walking along the path that ran by his cabin. To her relief, she saw plenty of evidence that he was still in residence but not once, no matter how she varied the time of her passing by, did she see him.

Then, one day when she'd just about reconciled herself to the fact that she'd have the beach all to herself for the remainder of her holiday, he showed up. Her physical reaction to the sight of him both shocked and mystified her. Her heart missed a beat, then made up for the omission by galloping out of control. *Frissons* of tension feathered over her skin, and she felt flustered—an unaccustomed experience as a rule but something that seemed to happen with puzzling frequency whenever she was confronted by him.

"I thought you'd moved on," she said, joining him at the water's edge. It was a blustery day and she'd dressed in jeans and a light cashmere sweater, but he seemed unaffected by the weather and wore his denim cutoffs and a black T-shirt.

He spared her one of his brief and scornful glances. "No, you didn't. You've been checking up on me with predictable regularity almost every day. I could have set my watch by your visits."

"If you're suggesting I've been looking through your window again, I hate to disappoint you but I'm afraid you're mistaken. I haven't set foot on your property."

"Technically, no," he agreed with a faint grin. "You left a little nose print behind after your first visit, and it's still there in lonely isolation. But you've been tempted."

"You wish!"

"How old are you, Laura Mitchell?"

"That's none of your business. Why do you want to know?"

"Because you ought to have outgrown blushing by now, yet you do it all the time, especially when you're not telling the truth. Some men might find it endearing, I suppose."

"But not you," Laura said resentfully, and stared out at the driftwood and kelp being hurled toward the shore by the incoming tide.

"Actually," he admitted, "you can be quite attractive at times—when you forget to be bossy and aggressive, that is."

"And you," she retorted, "no doubt prefer your women to be meek and submissive."

"Since you're not one of them, does it really matter what I prefer?"

She dared not answer. It shouldn't hurt to hear him speak such an obvious truth but, to her startled dismay, tears threatened.

What was it about Jackson Connery, a man so at odds with life in general that he could barely exchange a civil word with anyone, that he was able to arouse such a wanting in her? It wasn't as if they shared a thing in common. He was hostile and rude, a diamond in the rough at best. And at twenty-eight she ought to be past silly infatuations based on nothing more substantial than raw animal magnetism.

This wouldn't do at all! Laura blinked, and made a game of counting the darker patches of wood and kelp floating in the waves, hoping the exercise would restore her control.

As though he sensed her hurt and regretted being the cause of it, he startled her by taking her hand and spreading her fingers wide. "You're not married," he observed, tracing a line along her ring finger, "nor engaged. Is there someone special waiting for you, wherever it is you live?"

She shook her head, focusing on something out there, just beyond the breaking surf. Unlike the other flotsam being washed ashore, it seemed to be resisting the pull of the tide.

When he spoke next, his voice had taken on an edge that had been missing before. "What's the matter, Laura? What do you see?"

She sensed he was staring at her, but her earlier concern that he might notice her discomposure was eroded by a deeper fear. "I think there's a body out there," she said, the words almost choking her.

"Where?" His grip on her hand tightened painfully.

She found it oddly reassuring. He might be as alien to her way of life as someone from another planet, but not for a moment did she doubt his ability to take charge of the present situation. "There," she said, her voice cracking with dread. "See it?"

"No, damn it, I don't! Be specific."

"To your right, about two o'clock. Oh, *there*, you must have seen it then! It rode the crest of the wave for a second."

"Yes." Infected by her urgency, he started forward, dragging her along behind. "It's small—too small to be human, unless..."

"It could be a child," she whispered, reading his thoughts.

"It would have to be a baby, which is most unlikely," he said roughly. "Watch it, Laura. Don't take your eyes off it for a minute. I'm going in after it, but the current is fierce today. Whatever it is might get swept under and I'll need you to point to where I should search."

Apprehension held her in a merciless grip. "Be careful, Jackson!"

He heard her fear and shook her not ungently. "Listen," he said, bringing his face close to hers and immobilizing her with the sheer force of his determination, "this isn't the time for you to fall apart. You keep a lid on that panic until we've finished what we have to do, do you hear me?"

"It might be dead," she whimpered.

"Yes," he said, "it might. Does that relieve us of any responsibility?"

He was not a man who'd ever let her look away from the truth, no matter how unpleasant it might be. She closed her eyes briefly. "No."

"Well, then!" As he spoke, he stripped off his T-shirt and sneakers, dropped his denim cutoffs to the sand, but hastily this time, with none of that lazy, insolent grace that had hypnotized her before. "Wish me luck."

He was a strong swimmer and there was no reason for her to fear for him, yet she found herself holding her breath as he disappeared beneath an oncoming wave. What if *he* ended up needing to be rescued, too? She hadn't the strength to fight the current, let alone haul a man of his size to shore, and by the time she'd run up to the house for help it could be too late.

The relief when she saw him surface and shake back his hair almost made her eyes fill with tears again. She ran along the sand, paralleling his progress in the turbulent water. About fifty feet away, the object of his search curved over the top of a wave and was sucked out of sight. "Hurry!" she screamed, waving both arms.

He couldn't hear her, she knew, but he understood. He cut through the water as though the mere idea of failure was foreign to him. Then he disappeared again, and was out of sight for so long that she found herself praying, "Oh, please, God! Please, God!" over and over again. When Jackson came up for air some twenty yards from where he'd dived down, the relief that flooded through her almost outstripped her alarm for that other poor thing out there.

Contrarily, the sun chose that moment to slide out from behind a cloud, blinding her. Shading her eyes with her hand, she scanned the water, searching the faceted waves for a darker patch, a shape, any clue at all that would end the nightmare. She'd almost given up hope when she saw it again, even farther to the right and in danger of being flung on to the rocks near the far headland.

"Jackson!" She raced across the sand, trying not to lose sight of the tiny body that seemed to grow smaller with each passing second. "Jackson, over here!" Her throat grew raw from shouting, but he couldn't hear, he couldn't see, he wasn't understanding.

She was up to her knees in the water and not even aware of the cold, or the heavy denim of her jeans slowing her down. Jackson rode high on a wave, surfing and propelling himself along with powerful strokes of his arms, his eyes searching the water and this time finding what it was he sought. At the same time, she saw it again, too, inert now, no longer fighting, and only about fifty feet from the rocks.

Jackson drove himself forward and she kept pace with him, the water soaking her to the hips. He drew close and was sucked back by the current. For every two yards he gained he lost one, but somehow he closed in on his pathetic quarry.

She saw his hands reach out and pluck the body out of danger. She watched him fight for its safe return to shore, and his own. She didn't care that she was crying openly, sobbing his name and holding out her arms as if she were welcoming home a long-lost lover.

He waded ashore, shaking the water from his body. His chest was heaving and he cradled a dark bundle next to him. His hands were gentle and sorrowful, his face closed with emotion. "Look the other way, for

God's sake," he rasped between breaths, and tried to shield her from seeing.

It wasn't human, but it was a baby—a seal so small that it fitted in the crook of his arm. The little thing hung limply in his hold, its eyes closed. "Ah, Jackson!" Laura's tears stopped, dammed up by sorrow too acute to find such easy relief. "What happened to it?"

"I don't know."

She clung to his arm, struggling to keep up with him as he staggered up the beach. "Is it alive?"

"Barely." Tenderly, he laid the poor thing down on the sand. "Look, if you want to help, spread out my shirt so that I can wrap him up."

"What will we do then?"

"I'll take him to the cabin, and you'll go up to your house and phone——"

"Who? Who'll know what we should do?"

"The Vancouver Aquarium. Call them, tell them we've found a seal—a harbor seal, I think—and that it's tiny. Get them to give you directions about the——"

"He's opened his eyes!" Laura interrupted on an awed breath. "Oh, Jackson, he *is* alive! Look at his beautiful big eyes."

He brushed aside her wonder. "Listen to what I'm telling you. This is important if we're to save him."

As he spoke, he lifted the seal into his arms again and cushioned it next to his chest. As though it recognized its savior, the baby emitted a weak cry, a long drawn-out "Ma-ma-ma" that sounded almost human. "Well, I'll be damned," Jackson murmured hoarsely.

"I know you're not the kind of man who cries," Laura sobbed unashamedly, "so I hope you won't mind if I do it for both of us."

"Get moving and make that phone call," he said brusquely, and turned away. "Go on! Crying isn't going to accomplish anything! Tell them it weighs about twenty pounds, and that it doesn't have any injuries that we can see, but that it seems frail."

It took her almost half an hour, every minute of which seemed like a small eternity, but at last she was put through to the marine mammal department at the Aquarium. The biologist she spoke to gave her a sheaf of directions, solid, practical advice that she barely needed to write down because it seemed to imprint itself on her memory. But she made notes anyway, as anxious as any mother with a sick baby.

"Child," Honey Bee begged, as Laura hung up the phone, "if there's anything I can do, just tell me."

"Actually, there is something." Laura paused in her rummaging through the laundry cupboards for old blankets that could be used to make up a bed. "We give the baby a broad spectrum antibiotic, twice daily, the man suggested, for about five days, just to be on the safe side. But there's no vet up here. The nearest one's about eighty miles down the coast and only comes to town once a week."

"I'll call Dr. Barrow. I've been his patient long enough for him to trust me on this one and write out a prescription. Then I'll get Frank to drive into Pearce and pick up the medication from the clinic as soon as possible. What else?"

"We need a supply of some sort of infant formula that doesn't contain lactose—Enfalac, he said, or Prosobee, because they won't cause an allergic reaction. And vitamins—I don't know which kind, I forgot to ask, but I expect the sort they give human babies."

"Do you need a bottle to feed it?" Honey Bee stuffed a bag with beach towels and an old pillow and handed it to her.

Laura raked her fingers through her hair. "I didn't think to ask, but I guess not because he said to make the mixture thick like a milkshake—which reminds me, we have to get hold of some ground fish, too."

"Someone on the dock will help with that." For as long as Laura could remember, Honey Bee had always been dependable in an emergency. "Frank will see to it, my love. You get back to give that fine young man a hand and make sure he doesn't try to feed his seal cow's milk. You haven't come this far to lose the poor creature now."

Laura thought, when she arrived at the bottom of the porch steps, that she'd left it too late. There was no sign of Jackson, or the baby seal. But the door to the cabin stood open, and she must have made some noise that alerted him to her arrival because he called out, "Come on in, Laura Mitchell. This is one time you don't have to stand outside and look through the window."

He lay propped on his side on the cot with the seal curled up next to him. Halfway through the door, Laura came to an abrupt halt. "Good heavens, your bed is going to smell dreadful, Jackson!"

"Never mind that. What did you find out?"

He'd changed into a soft gray flannel shirt and a pair of Levi's that stopped just short of fitting too snugly. Grateful to have her attention directed away from the sight, Laura recited directions, explaining that Frank had been sent into Pearce for the things they'd need and would bring them straight to the cabin.

"Judging from its weight, the little thing's probably not more than a couple of days old," she finished, approaching the bed. "The biologist thought the mother was probably eaten by a killer whale or killed by fishermen, and warned me that this little guy won't be able to fend for himself until he's been weaned and taught to catch his own fish."

"Sounds as if we've got our work cut out for us for the next few weeks." Jackson looked up from stroking the sleek fur. For the first time, his eyes were without their habitual reserve and he smiled at her with real warmth. "Are you planning to stick around for a while?"

She felt herself drowning in his gaze. "For a while, at any rate," she managed, and snatched a breath. "What—um—what are you going to call him?"

"Charlie," he said without hesitation.

He sounded so proud that she laughed. "Any particular reason for your choice?"

"Because it's a good name for a boy." He moved over a few inches and patted the cot invitingly. "Come and stroke him. He feels like silk."

The mattress sagged a little beneath her weight, and she found herself sliding toward Jackson. His knee nudged hers, his thigh grazed her hip—innocuously on his part, she was sure, but the heat rolled over her in smothering waves. She flinched.

His eyes narrowed in amusement. "It's okay," he said. "He won't bite, and neither will I. What did the guy have to say about keeping him wet?"

"It's not really necessary," she replied, clutching the frame of the bed in order to preserve a little more space between them. "He should be kept in a well-ventilated place, out of direct sunlight and secure from other animals. If you want to hose him down occasionally, he'll probably enjoy it but don't be surprised if he decides he'd rather live in here with you. The chances are he'll adopt you as his mother and won't let you out of his sight. He's looking for someone to bond with."

Jackson didn't look displeased at the idea. "He's fallen asleep," he said, stroking the small head. "Poor little devil! I think we found him just in time."

"You're the one who saved him," Laura said quietly. "If it had been up to me, I'd never have been able to bring him in."

"But you're the one who spotted him first," Jackson reminded her, and there was a gentleness in him that she'd never found before, as though the baby brought out all that was best in him, leaving no room for the anger that so often seemed to drive him. For once, he seemed happy, all his sharp edges smoothed away. "We did it together."

They spoke in whispers, and smiled at each other, like parents full of awe at the miracle they'd produced. The atmosphere almost quivered and, out of the blue, Laura found there were holes in the perfect interweaving of emotional and professional satisfaction that had been her life until that moment.

She didn't think she was a shallow woman, yet all at once it seemed as though she'd done her living on the fringes and let what really mattered pass her by. The woman who had always been grateful for all the good and wonderful things she had, all at once found herself wishing for things she had not. She'd never experienced first hand the passion of union, the mutual and absolute trust of a man and a woman coming together to design something uniquely theirs. And suddenly she wanted them so intensely that her heart ached and it hurt to breathe.

Rescuing Charlie was only a facsimile of the real thing. The warmth, the sense of sharing, of having created something lasting and wonderful was a temporary pleasure that would end with summer. Unless . . . no, it was unthinkable!

But she was thinking it, regardless. What would it be like to be close to Jackson? Not in love with him, because, of course, that would be asking for a miracle, all things considered—but to have him as a lover, just for a little while?

The biggest mistake she could make, that was what! They were a man and woman too selfishly protecting their feelings to dare reveal their private needs. Yet, when the dark afternoon closed around them, it seemed that fate was intervening, disguising the cabin and turning it into a place of special intimacy and refuge in which to make reparation for each other's omissions.

"You're soaking wet," Jackson said, fingering the stuff of her jeans. "Why didn't you change while you were up at the house?"

"I forgot," she said. "There were more important things to worry about."

"I could light a fire." His hand rested on her thigh, lightly, possessively. "You could dry off while we wait for the supplies to get here."

She could hardly speak for the sensations coursing through her. "That would be nice."

Squatting before the hearth, he struck a match to the kindling laid ready. The flames crept along, quiet little flickers of light that suddenly flared into crackling life.

He reached for the sleeping bag folded neatly across the foot of the cot. "Cover up with this and get out of those damp clothes," he invited, holding it out like a cape. "You're shivering."

She was, but not from the cold. He couldn't know, as she wriggled free of her jeans and wrapped herself in the sleeping bag, that she was wishing he was the reason she was stripping away her clothing. Why couldn't he be more intuitive, instead of shrouding himself in all this mystery and reserve?

Curiosity and the particular insanity he always evoked got the better of her. "Who are you, really?" she asked, joining him by the flames and drawing her finger over the hard planes of his face from his cheekbone to the corner of his mouth. His jaw was lightly bearded, as though he hadn't shaved that morning.

His eyes flared, their blue depths turning molten. "Take your hand away," he muttered, and turned his head aside.

She didn't enjoy rejection and seldom made the first overtures. It would have been more in character for her to jump up and leave him to his orphaned seal and his solitude, but she couldn't bring herself to obey either his order or the dictates of her own good sense.

Events had conspired to bring her face-to-face with a truth that lay rooted in a more ancient wisdom than that by which she'd previously lived. It confronted him, too. She could see it in his eyes, even though he fought hard to deny it. The tendons of his neck stood out in sharp relief as though a very slender margin of control was all that prevented him from succumbing to the temptations she offered.

Maybe that was what gave her courage. Ignoring his command, she swept her hand lightly through the mass of his hair. It spilled in thick disorder through her fingers, highlighted to palest gold where the fire's reflection caught it. She heard him draw in a sharp breath and his fingers came up to halt hers.

"Cut it out, Laura, unless you're prepared to deal with the consequences."

"And if I am, then what?"

"I'm not your type," he said in a hard voice.

She'd have agreed with him a week ago—an hour ago, even. But now? "How do you know?" She cupped his jaw in the palm of her hand and forced him to look at her.

"Little fool," he said, and she saw his chest rise and fall shallowly. "You're about as well suited to playing the siren as that baby over there is capable of fending for himself in the wild."

He was right. She'd been too busy with other things to worry about her lack of experience in matters of romance. Now, here she was, emotions and needs stripped bare in a way she'd never before known, by a man she'd never expected could touch her so deeply, and she hadn't the first idea of how to deal with any of it. At twenty-eight she was still a novice in the art of seduction.

At that moment, however, it didn't seem to matter. Instinct stepped in where experience fell short and took over without a qualm. "Teach me, then," she whispered, and slid her hand inside his open shirt.

His chest was firm, its contours sharply defined. A light dusting of hair skimmed abrasively against the pads of her fingertips. And even she knew what his racing heart signified. He was no more indifferent to her than was she to him.

She abhorred violence and had no use for women who subjected themselves to it in the name of love. Yet, when he tried to shove her away, she clung to him with such strength and determination that they both went sprawling. She ought to have felt shame, but knew not a second's embarrassment. Her only awareness was the wild belief that this man could chase away the gnawing emptiness that had haunted her of late.

She was filled with the scent of him, a spicy fragrance combined of salt air and cedar and pure, clean masculinity. Even though he supported his weight on his hands, it did nothing to subvert the intimacy of his limbs twined with hers. She had likened him to a god, a savage, and any number of other beings, not all of them flattering, but nothing could disguise the fact that he was merely a man, at the mercy of his body's responses whether he liked it or not. His texture and shape were eloquent with a passion he seemed almost to despise, as though to be so needy was a weakness he refused to allow himself.

"This is a mistake," he muttered, but his lips denied the allegation and closed on hers with potent hunger.

Nobody had ever kissed her like that—beguilingly and with such finesse that her mouth softened and invited him in. It wasn't just symbolic. Everything she had to offer was his for the taking.

The sleeping bag fell away, reshaping itself to a mattress. The fire settled with a sigh and bathed them in a quiet glow. Laura felt all the inhibitions that had kept her pure as driven snow for so many years begin to crumble and that cold, hard lump of loneliness inside melted in the warmth to let passion loose with a vengeance.

His hand slipped down her arm, tangled with her fingertips, slid to her bare thigh. His touch seared her flesh, sparking impulses of pleasure and leaving those parts he'd not yet discovered screaming for appeasement.

She did something then that would have shocked her at any other time. She reached for his hand and placed it on her breast. Even without words, she thought the agony of need that consumed her must surely communicate itself to him. She was on fire, and helpless to put out the flames. Desire raged, an aching pressure that refused to be satisfied with anything less than complete fulfillment.

She dared to open her eyes, and saw torment on his face, as though he wrestled with devils she couldn't begin to comprehend. "What, Jackson?" she implored on a ragged breath. "What is it? What am I doing wrong?"

He shook his head, scrunching his eyes shut, and rolled away from her. A groan escaped him, so full of pain that she wished she were not so untutored. It seemed selfish to want so much and be able to offer so little in return, but it wasn't lack of generosity that held her back—it was ignorance of how best to please him.

She placed her hand on his chest again, and when he didn't rebuff her she grew bolder, unbuttoning his shirt and pulling it free from the waist of his Levi's. She'd seen him with far fewer clothes and had marveled at the sight, but the feel of him enthralled her beyond anything she could have imagined. He possessed a refinement and grace of form thoroughly at odds with the image he worked so hard to preserve. This was not a backwoodsman, governed by crude instinct; this was an aristocrat in disguise.

His stomach was flat and hard, his hips lean. Full of wonder at the power and strength of him, she stared at her hand as it traversed his ribs and strayed past his waist into forbidden territory. She wanted to feel all of him pressed against her, and refused to allow false modesty to deter her. Hypocrisy had no place in what was happening between them.

"Stop!" The word tore out of his mouth like gravel flung against crystal. Harsh, shattering. His fingers around her wrists numbed her with their determination.

"No!" Less an objection than a plea, her voice echoed plaintively through the room.

It seemed to infuriate him. He leapt to his feet and flung her damp jeans at her. "Get dressed," he raged, tucking in his own shirt, "and quit flaunting your skinny endowments at me. I like my women well covered."

If he had stabbed her, she thought it would have hurt her less. He made her feel cheap and pathetic, neither lady enough to keep her emotions under control, nor woman enough to satisfy him. She scrambled into her clothes and tossed the sleeping bag onto the foot of the cot, shame scalding her face.

He spun on his heel, as though he couldn't stand the sight of her, and strode to the window. "The supplies just arrived," he informed her, and took off out the door and down the steps, leaving her a few blessed moments in which to compose herself.

Frank was not a loquacious man. By the time Laura came outside, too, he was already heading back along the bluff to Honey Bee's house.

"If you hurry, you can catch up with him," Jackson said in that same cold, indifferent tone he'd used the first day he'd spoken to her. "I can manage by myself now."

Well, damn him!

Gathering her wounded pride around her like a shield, Laura sought to return her hurt in full measure but was able to come up with only a feeble insult. "You're not the only one," she spat. "It'll be a cold day in hell before I bother you again."

## CHAPTER FOUR

JACKSON wished he could believe her. He wished Laura could tell him she found him repugnant, the antithesis of everything she respected and desired in a man, and mean it. It would have hurt him less, and God only knew how much it would have spared her. But, even after everything that had happened to him in the last two years, cruelty wasn't something he enjoyed, and he'd been cruel with her. He'd seen bewilderment cloud her eyes, watched the tenderness seared by a shame she should never have had to know, and it had almost killed him not to take her in his arms again and beg her forgiveness.

"Ahhh!" Enraged with things he couldn't change, he slammed a fist into the post supporting the porch and wished the sky would fall down and bury him. How had this happened? How was it that, in all the wild and lonely miles of coast in British Columbia, he'd chosen this particular spot to try to find himself again?

Nursing his bruised hand, he glared at the heavens. "I don't deserve this sort of punishment!" he bellowed. "And neither does she!"

It was time to move on. His well-honed instincts for survival had been telling him that practically from the moment she first showed up on the beach. He'd ignored them, told himself he wasn't going to let a slip of a woman drive him away from the first real haven of peace and privacy he'd known in years. He'd told himself he could withstand the lure of her clear, wide-eyed gaze because only a fool would believe he could sink into their green depths without drowning, and he'd outgrown being a fool a long time ago.

Or so he'd thought. Because if he was so smart, how the hell was it that he was still here, not footloose and free to roam as he'd thought, but mired in complications that were multiplying by the hour?

"Charlie," he muttered, searching for infant formula in the box of supplies on the table, "I hope you survive to appreciate the risks I'm running because of you."

The seal lifted his head. "Ma . . . ma . . . ma . . ." he whimpered.

If someone had told her that she'd welcome her mother's arrival at Carter's Cove, Laura would have scoffed. Whatever else her shortcomings, however, Rose was always a distraction, and Laura badly needed distraction in the days that followed.

Of course, any semblance of peace or harmony flew out of the window the minute Rose drew up at the front door in her white Mercedes convertible. "Grandmother," she pouted, chiffon scarves floating, "that road should be blasted to perdition! It's a threat to life and limb, and God only knows what it's done to the paint on my car. Laura, darling, I expected you'd be here again."

"Lovely to see you, too, Mother," Laura replied dryly, and prised herself loose from Rose's embrace. Too much kissing the air in the vicinity of each other's cheeks turned her stomach.

"Stop fussing over the car and come inside," Honey Bee said. "For heaven's sake, Rose, the thing isn't going to melt, and if imported craftsmanship is everything it's reputed to be your paint will be none the worse for the journey. How are you?"

"Rather frazzled." Rose exhaled a mournful sigh and flipped open a gold powder compact to examine her face. "The dust and the glare are so hard on one's complexion."

"I'm sure a glass of wine will restore you," Honey Bee remarked wryly. "Frank will take up your bags, so leave your things and come out to the patio and join us in a drink before lunch. Isn't Laura looking wonderful?"

Rose turned critical eyes Laura's way. "Robust, certainly, with all that brown skin. Is that a Liz Claiborne blouse, Laura?"

"Jones, New York, actually. Honey Bee, shall I pour the wine?"

"Thank you, my love, that would be nice."

It was a very fine Australian Chardonnay. Rose wrinkled her nose and said, "Not exactly Moët et Chandon, is it? Still running your little gallery, Laura?"

"Yes."

"And still single, with no prospects on the horizon?"

"You'll be one of the first to hear differently, Mother, if that ever changes."

"You're nearly thirty, Laura."

"In my prime, Mother."

Rose shrugged mystified, silk-clad shoulders. "I'd think your age would worry you."

From inside the house, the phone rang. "You worry enough for both of us, Mother. Honey Bee, shall I bring the phone out here?"

"No, I'll take it inside." Honey Bee rose from her chair before Rose could rush over and help. "I'm expecting a call from that incompetent broker of mine. Excuse me, won't you?"

"Of course, Grandmother." Rose hovered until Honey Bee was out of earshot, then turned to Laura. "What do you suppose she has to discuss with her broker that can't be said in front of us?"

"Honey Bee's money matters are her own affair, Mother. There's no reason she should feel she has to share them with us."

The barb hit the mark. Rose flushed and changed the subject. "Why can't you call her Great-Grandmother, like any normal person, for God's sake?" she demanded peevishly. "All this 'Honey Bee' stuff is enough to make a person ill."

"It was my great-grandfather's pet name for her."

"That was his misfortune. Do you have to make it yours?"

"I happen to think it suits her," Laura said, swirling the wine in her glass, and forbore to add that "waspish" suited Rose even better. She could only assume, from her mother's nervous tension, that all was not progressing well with the latest suitor. "How long are you planning to stay?"

"Not a minute longer than I have to, darling, you can be sure. Country living isn't my style." Rose stretched out on a chaise and eyed Laura appraisingly. "You know, Laura, it's all very fine for you to be so high-minded about independence but there'll come a time when you're not quite so full of energy and youth, and you might wish then that you'd made more of an effort to secure a husband when you had the chance."

Laura rolled her eyes. "Considering the speed with which you discard yours, Mother, I can only assume they aren't worth the chase. Can we talk about something else? The national debt, perhaps, or global warming?"

"Dear me, I've produced an intellectual." Rose's smile bore the bewildered air of a bird of paradise discovering a common sparrow in its nest. "Is it my imagination, darling, or are you being particularly testy today?"

"I'm sorry, Mother." She was, too. She would have preferred to enjoy Rose's company, and if that was asking too much, considering their different attitudes and personalities, then she would have been glad to settle for amicable tolerance. But, as usual, Rose had put her on the defensive and they both ended up saying cruel, insensitive things to each other. Honey Bee was right. It wasn't natural.

"What is it?" Rose leaned forward, a certain avid hope in her eyes. "Are you worried about your great-grandmother? Isn't she well?"

"I'm fine, Rose, and plan to live until I'm a hundred and one," Honey Bee declared, returning to the patio on silent feet. "Laura, my love, you have a visitor. Rose, this is Mr. Connery, my neighbor."

He was wearing the more respectable jeans, and a white shirt Laura had never seen before, with its sleeves rolled up to show strong, tanned forearms. His hair was damp, and he was freshly shaved, but Laura was too astonished by his arrival to pay more than cursory attention to his spruced-up appearance. "Jackson, what are you doing here? Has something happened to Charlie?" she asked.

"No," he said. "I came to see you."

"I tried to talk him into joining us for lunch," Honey Bee put in, "but I didn't have much luck. Maybe you can persuade him, Laura."

He dwarfed the patio and the mere fact of his presence had the atmosphere humming. Briefly acknowledging Rose, he turned his attention to Honey Bee. "Thank you, ma'am. At any other time, I'd be more than delighted, but I do need to speak alone with Laura today."

"Then pour yourself a glass of wine, young man, and let my great-granddaughter show you my orchids. You can have all the privacy you need in the conservatory."

Situated on the east side of the house to catch the morning sun, the conservatory was far enough away that nothing they had to say to each other was likely to be overheard.

"Well?" By the time the door was shut behind them, Laura had had time to remember how cruel he'd been the last time they'd seen each other. "What makes you think I want to hear anything you have to say, Jackson?"

"Telling you I'm sorry hardly cuts it, I suppose, but I want you to know that I regret speaking to you the way I did the other day."

Not, "I didn't mean what I said," which might have stroked her ego a little, but "I regret having been so blunt." "I can't think of a nice way to tell someone you find them totally unattractive," she said.

"I think we both know I didn't find you unattractive."

Past tense. A momentary madness, brought on by the euphoria of having saved an orphaned seal.

Disappointment knifed through her. For all that she should have known better, she'd allowed herself the tiny hope that he'd come to say he hadn't been able to get her off his mind. Why? He was just a man, after all.

She buried a sigh. Ah, yes, but *such* a man!

"Well," she said, hoping that he wasn't perceptive enough to see past her bravado to the hurt underneath, "now that you've got that off your chest, is there anything else?"

"Apologies have a habit of confusing the real issue," he said, "and I'm a bit out of practice when it comes to diplomacy, but——"

"Accusing me of flaunting myself amounts to something more than lack of diplomacy," she flung at him, goaded into ignoring her resolve to preserve an unmoved front. "I'd say that comes closer to pure cruelty."

His knuckles gleamed white around the slender stem of his wineglass. "I had to put a stop to what was happening."

"Well, a simple 'No, thanks' would have done the job." She glared at him, renewed anger and pain combining to make her reckless. "You didn't have to add insult to injury by telling me I'm not exactly voluptuous. Or did you perhaps think I needed your epicurean eye to point out something my mirror's been telling me ever since I graduated from kneesocks?"

"I find you lovely," he said, "and eminently desirable."

"Don't make fun of me!" She dashed away the silly tears.

He swore, and set down his glass in a prize cymbidium. "Listen——"

"No. Go away."

The lengthy silence that followed persuaded her that he'd done as she asked. She thought it was safe to cry but, instead of a flood of tears, a dry, painful sob emerged.

His hands on her shoulders were gentle. "Laura, look at me."

"Stop being kind," she muttered, flinching at his touch. "I'm not an infant seal in need of rescue."

"You're not in need of anyone," he said, "especially not a man like me. I did you a favor when I stopped making love to you."

"Then please don't do me any more favors," she begged with unalloyed sarcasm, "because you don't know the first thing about what I need."

"Perhaps not," he said, "but I know what I see when I look at you."

His glance roamed over her. Warm as morning sunlight, it touched her hips, inched past her waist to her breasts and hesitated there as though moved by a special memory, then slid up her neck to her face. For a moment that stretched into two and then three he looked deep into her eyes.

Then he shook his head as though to unclutter his mind of irrelevant details. "You're an attractive, well-put-together young woman with all the right curves in all the right places. There must be a——"

"You called them skinny endowments before," she reminded him, and scrubbed at the tear that succeeded in drizzling down her face. "You said you liked your women well covered."

"And, despite all the evidence to the contrary, you believed me." He sighed, as though he'd run a long and grueling race without winning, and shook her lightly. "What am I going to do about you?"

His touch was not overtly sexy or suggestive in the way most women might have preferred, but she'd never been like most women, and all that mattered now was that the contact of his rough palms on her skin stirred her unbearably. It made her say things she'd normally have kept to herself. "Why do you have to do anything? Why can't you just let things happen naturally, let what will be, be?"

"Because it would be disastrous." He nudged her chin so that her face tilted up to his. "Take a good look at me, then tell me, if you can, what we have in common."

His eyebrows had stolen tiny flecks of gold from his hair. His nose was straight, his ears neat and flat against his skull. Beyond that she dared not go. The temptation to touch was too strong. "Nothing anyone can see, perhaps," she said, her breath ricocheting past the words, "but there's something between us. I sense it, and I know that you do, too."

"You don't know what you're talking about," he insisted. "We come from different worlds. I'm all wrong for a woman like you."

She made the mistake of looking at his mouth. It reminded her of the way his kisses had warmed her lips and she couldn't bear to think she'd never experience the pleasure again. Hurriedly, she slid her gaze over the high planes of his cheekbones. "You're just making excuses," she whispered, hypnotized by the way his lashes drooped lower with each word she spoke. "I'm old enough to decide for myself what's right for me."

"And what's that?" he inquired, his question skimming over her mouth.

The last thing she saw before her own eyes fell shut was the blue intensity of his. "This," she sighed and, succumbing to temptation, threaded her fingers through his thick blond hair, and pulled his head down so that she could kiss him one more time.

Just for a moment, he weakened. His lips tasted her, and came back for a second helping. His hands stole up her throat to cradle her jaw.

She tried telling herself that she'd been touched by summer madness, that to allow herself to get caught up in such sweeping emotion was to invite chaos into her life, but a little moan of pure bliss escaped her. He didn't feel like the wrong man for her at all. He felt exactly, perfectly right.

Unhappily, he seemed not to agree. "No," he muttered against her mouth. "This isn't what you need."

She pulled away just far enough to look at him through eyes grown slumbrous with desire. "What is, Jackson?"

He sighed as though beset by more problems than any one man should have to solve without divine intervention, and dipped his mouth to hers again. "Friendship, perhaps? Maybe if we stopped fighting, we wouldn't feel compelled to go to the opposite extreme either, and could settle for something in between."

"Friends," she whispered, "don't kiss like this."

"No," he agreed, and loosened his arms so that they slid down her shoulders to loop around her waist. "We'll have to keep a tighter rein..."

His lips lingered, bestowed, withdrew a fraction. The taste of Chardonnay had never been so intoxicating. "Yes," she sighed.

"After all, you'll be gone soon..."

"Yes."

"And I'll stay here or move on..."

Orchids had no scent so it must be his hair sifting through her fingers that smelled so sweet. "Where to?"

He shrugged massively, and the aftershock rolled up her breasts and down again. "Wherever. I'm not interested in putting down roots, whereas you——"

"I'm a career woman," she finished for him. "I've got different priorities. You're right: no two people were ever more unsuited."

That concession finally broke the spell. He put her from him, leaving a chill emptiness to fill the space he'd previously occupied. "Exactly. You're a nice woman, Laura, but you're not my type of woman and never will be."

"I know," she agreed, and wondered why it felt as if he'd just cut out her heart.

Honey Bee took one look at Laura's face and didn't press him to stay. "I realize you have a baby to feed, Mr. Connery, and ought to be getting back, but it's a shame you have to miss my housekeeper's excellent bouillabaisse. Can I persuade you to take some home? I think both you and Charlie would enjoy it."

"I'm sure we would, Mrs. Carter. He's getting as tired of my cooking as I am."

The warmth of the smile he bestowed on Honey Bee sent such a shaft of pain through Laura's heart that she wished he hadn't bothered to come back to take his leave in person. Rose, however, remained singularly unimpressed. "You have a son whom you call Charlie?" she inquired, wrinkling her nose. She didn't hold with abbreviating fine old names.

"A young seal," Jackson said.

"Seal?" Rose could barely contain her amusement. "You mean one of those dear little sea creatures that make such lovely fur jackets?"

Jackson looked at Rose, and his eyes were flat and cold in a way Laura had never seen before. "The very same," he said, "but I do assure you, ma'am, that Charlie will never end up on some rich woman's back."

Laura knew Jackson well enough to sense his outrage but Rose, oblivious to the tension, stepped ever more carelessly onto the already thin ice. "And you're planning to waste bouillabaisse on this animal? In case you aren't aware, Mr. Connery, bouillabaisse is the French term for a classical and very fine fish dish——"

"Mother," Laura interjected, anxious to avoid an unpleasant scene.

Jackson silenced her with a look. Don't run interference for me, it said. I can fight my own battles. "And in Italy," he purred, swinging his gaze to Rose again, "something similar is called *cioppino*."

Rose gaped for a second then brought her jaws together with a decisive click. "How illuminating! Do you read cookbooks as a hobby?"

"Rose!" Halfway out of her chair, Honey Bee clutched the table, her face masked in rare annoyance. "Mr. Connery is a welcome guest in my home and I expect you to treat him accordingly."

She accepted Jackson's arm and smiled apologetically. "Come with me, Mr. Connery," she invited, "and I'll introduce you to Wanda, my housekeeper. But don't think that a take-home lunch today excuses you from accepting my earlier invitation to dinner. I expect to see you again in my home some time very soon."

He was barely out of earshot before the inquisition began. "Laura!" Rose sat on the edge of her chair, agog with curiosity. "Where *did* you find the savage?"

"On the beach, Mother, and he's not so savage that he didn't outwit you at your little game of one-upmanship."

As usual when she found herself outflanked in an argument with her daughter, Rose attacked on a different front. "Your lipstick's smudged," she said lightly. "If I didn't know better, I'd think you kissed the frog in the hope he'd turn into a prince."

Laura did her best not to betray her discomfiture. "That's ridiculous."

"Isn't it?" Rose's Tinkerbell laugh chimed merrily. "And yet you're blushing, darling. Such a quaint habit, I've always thought, and so revealing! One might almost suspect you find all that manly brawn attractive."

Laura thought about the various responses open to her, decided she'd be less likely to incriminate herself if she kept quiet, and hoped her mother might feel disposed to do likewise.

It was a vain hope. "He has a certain eccentric fascination, I suppose," Rose continued, "living alone in a shack with a pet seal for company. But one must surely question why."

"Not everyone has your extravagant tastes, Mother. There's nothing wrong with a simple life."

Rose's eyes narrowed. "But there's plenty wrong with being simpleminded," she snorted, "which is what you most assuredly must be if you're prepared to take him at face value. For pity's sake, Laura, I'd have thought you too sophisticated to let yourself be blinded to so obvious a fact."

Why was it, Laura wondered with a stifled sigh, that hearing the truth from Rose made it so much harder to accept?

Her mother left two days later, which was a relief. At least Laura didn't have to be on her guard all the time. If Honey Bee was disconcertingly observant, she was also sensitive enough to draw conclusions without feeling compelled to voice them, which left Laura free to wrestle with her demon in private, something she attempted to do for three whole days.

The demon, of course, was her heart, which insisted on going its contrary way despite her attempts to keep it in line. Never mind that she told herself a hundred times that Jackson was right when he said that they were about as mismatched a pair as two people could possibly be. Her heart simply refused to agree.

Be friends by all means, it whispered in the dark hours of the night. Friendship is nice, desirable even—but why stop there?

And that was utterly ridiculous because, quite apart from the fact that she and Jackson came from different worlds, the timing was all wrong for a serious involvement. Laura was perfectly happy with her life as it presently stood, and she would be much too busy in the coming months to have energy to spare for love, even if Jackson showed the least inclination to let matters go that far—which he didn't.

Furthermore, it was ridiculous even to entertain the idea that the currents swirling between her and Jackson amounted to something quite that durable or earthshaking. Love did not spring from physical attraction and an infatuation that was probably as fleeting as summer. It grew from deeply rooted affection sown over time, from shared interests and a thorough knowledge and understanding of each other. And the plain truth was, Laura knew next to nothing about Jackson and didn't understand him at all.

In fact, much as it galled her, she was forced to agree with Rose. There was something about him that didn't ring quite true, little inconsistencies that suggested he wasn't merely what he pretended to be.

He was well-spoken and articulate when he forgot to act the part in which he'd cast himself. The shirt he'd worn the day he appeared on Honey Bee's patio had been beautifully made and, unless she missed her guess, of one hundred per cent fine cotton. The books Laura had seen spread out on the table in his cabin were heavy, studious-looking tomes, as contradictory to the image he worked so hard to project as the handsomely designed frames of his glasses.

Most puzzling of all, however, was his refusal to let her scrape below the surface to discover the real person underneath the magnetic good looks and sex appeal. He was a man without a past whose reserve hid a lot more than mere shyness, and Laura's normal inclination to respect his privacy was offset by a perverse streak that demanded answers to the questions simmering in her mind.

It was this curiosity that finally convinced her to take him up on his offer of friendship. If he was sincere and really wanted them to be friends, he'd shed some insight on himself and provide some missing pieces to the puzzle.

And maybe, she rationalized, she would find she didn't like him nearly as much as she feared she might, once she got to know him better.

The next morning, with the temperature outside climbing toward eighty, she picked her way down the steps to the beach, determined to keep her emotions in check. Halfway down the cliff she stopped and let her gaze scan the width of the cove. Almost at once it settled on Jackson's tall frame down at the water's edge, and a stabbing pain skewered her heart. Before he'd so much as noticed her, he'd put to rout her entire plan of defense.

She might have turned and run back the way she'd come except that he looked up then and saw her hovering like a bird unsure of where to land. "Hey," he said amiably, strolling over to wait at the foot of the steps, "your timing's perfect. I just brought Charlie down for his first swim in the ocean since the day we fished him out."

If she'd hoped that almost a week's absence had magnified his charms out of all proportion to reality, she soon learned differently. When she looked at him, she didn't see a man at odds with the sort of life she led—she saw a man whose magnetic pull defied her most strenuous attempts to resist him.

His shoulders were every bit as wide as she remembered, his hair as thick and sun-bleached. He had on his swimming trunks, and while her tan had faded during the recent spell of bad weather his seemed to have deepened. The sky paled beside his eyes and the sun seemed cool compared with his smile. The whole world, in fact, lost a little bit of its grandeur.

"Well?" He held out his hand. "What do you say?"

Say no, the tiny voice of self-preservation warned her. Make up some excuse.

She looked at his hand, at the broad and callused palm, and knew that if she touched him once she'd be lost.

The strong fingers beckoned an invitation, luring her to take chances, even though the sanity that normally kept impulse in line warned her that he wasn't offering what her heart really craved. "Laura?"

But, in thrall to a compulsion she couldn't withstand, she placed her hand in his and wondered why the electricity that shot through her didn't fell both of them on the spot.

## CHAPTER FIVE

CHARLIE frolicked in the waves lapping at the beach. Fatter and sleeker, he was, if possible, more adorable than ever. Certainly, he was happier.

Glad of an excuse to extricate her hand from Jackson's, Laura knelt in the shallows and stroked the seal's smooth, domed head. "Good heavens, he's grown!"

"Babies have a habit of doing that, I understand." Jackson's voice was full of pride, his blue eyes alight with laughter. "There isn't room in my home-rigged shower for both of us any longer. He's definitely ready for bigger things."

As if to prove the point, Charlie performed a neat somersault, rolling into the waves and riding the surf with a grace that was almost balletic.

Jackson crouched next to Laura. "I thought it was about time I brought him down here. He's ready to broaden his horizons."

She flung him a doubtful glance. "You're not thinking of releasing him?"

"Not yet. He's too young to survive all by himself." He reached into a pail wedged between a couple of rocks and flung a small herring in the air. "Hey, Charlie, catch!"

The seal missed, gave a pathetic little bark, and fixed soulful eyes on Jackson.

"See what I mean? He won't be independent until he learns to do his own hunting."

"Even then, how will you be able to bear to let him go when you've hand-raised him since he was no more than a couple of days old?" Laura shook her head. "I know I couldn't, in your place."

Without meaning to, she touched a nerve. Jackson's sunny mood clouded over. "Then thank God you're not in my place," he declared with a scowl. "He's got a right to his freedom, and it goes against everything I believe in to keep him in captivity one single day longer than necessary. A man has to have a very good reason to do that to another living creature."

"Well, there are other alternatives, Jackson."

His disdain seared her. "Like a circus, perhaps, where he can learn to balance a ball on his nose?"

"No, like the Vancouver Aquarium where he'll be well cared for."

"I hate places like that."

"You were glad enough of their help the day Charlie got washed up on the beach," she reminded him, bracing herself for a fresh outburst of scorn.

He didn't disappoint her. "Using the facilities to look after sick and injured animals is one thing, but when they wind up as nothing more than a glorified holding pen——"

"You're shouting at me, Jackson."

He glowered at her, then looked a little shamefaced. "I guess I am," he admitted. "You seem to have that sort of effect on me."

"Meaning it's my fault the world hasn't been custom-created to your specifications, I suppose?"

"Yes—no! Oh, hell, didn't we agree we were going to try to be friends? Why is it so difficult for us to get along?"

"Friends usually aren't so ready to take offense where none's intended," Laura pointed out. "From the way you reacted just now, I thought perhaps you'd changed your mind and decided after all that you'd rather I kept to my side of the beach and left you to yours."

He looked at her long and seriously. "I—not exactly."

"But you have reservations?"

"If I have," he replied, shoving the pail toward her, "they have to do with me, not you. Why don't you toss Charlie a herring? Maybe he'll try harder to catch for you."

"I doubt it. You're the coach he's used to."

The trace of a grin resurfaced. "Yeah, but he probably thinks you're prettier."

"Flatterer!" But she was able to smile and even found herself relaxing a little. There was a very nice man under all that prickly reserve, and a summer friendship with him was precisely what she needed—*not* the complications of a romance, however fleeting.

"Well, I mean it. He's a smart little devil and there's no question that he's getting a bit bored with me and the same old routine." Jackson inched the pail closer. "Go on, give it a try. Grab a fish and throw it up in the air so that he can see it coming."

She peered dubiously into the pail. "You mean, pick up one of these things with my bare hands?"

It was the first time she'd heard him laugh like that, freely and without the habitual undercurrent of bitterness. "They're already dead, Laura. They won't bite."

"But they look . . . slimy."

"I bet you were one of those little girls who never got her hands dirty when she played." He shook his head ruefully. "I should have known."

"And I suppose you were a hellion."

"Yes." He nodded. "My mother claimed I was responsible for every gray hair in her head. Said she hoped I had sons of my own some day, just to even the score."

The image of a towheaded boy with summer blue eyes racing out to meet each new day, perhaps with a dog romping at his side, filled Laura's mind. "That's the first time you've ever volunteered anything about your past," she murmured, and knew right away that she'd presumed too much on their newborn friendship.

"Because the past isn't worth reliving," he said, his closed expression and cool, watchful gaze a sure sign that the barriers were in place again. If she pushed too hard, he would shut her out completely. Theirs was a now relationship, its past confined to a few select shared memories only and its future brief at best.

"You're right." Her own laugh, deliberately light and dismissive to hide a regret that she couldn't begin to fathom, made her throat ache. Why, when he was willing to give her exactly what she'd convinced herself she wanted, was her heart crying for the moon?

She reached into the pail and grasped one of the dead herring. It felt every bit as cold and unpleasant as she'd feared. "Ahh, yuck!" She let out a shriek and flung it into the ocean.

Charlie's attention fastened on the arcing flash of silver, and the next moment he reared up out of the waves and caught the fish deftly in his mouth.

"Now that," Jackson declared, his mood lightening perceptibly, "is grossly unfair. Beginner's luck, I'd call it, and I bet you can't do it a second time."

"I only gamble when I'm sure of winning, and I think I've pushed my luck far enough for one day." Laura rinsed her hands in the water then stood up. "Nice seeing you again, Charlie. Don't grow up too fast, okay?"

Jackson looked taken aback. "Hey, what do you think you're doing?"

Putting a little distance between us since that seems to be the only way I can think rationally, she was tempted to retort because, if she hadn't known better, she'd have thought those blue eyes were clouded with disappointment. "I brought along a book to keep me entertained. Being friends doesn't mean we have to live in each other's back pockets, after all."

"You can read any old time," he protested.

"No, I can't. Usually, I'm so busy that it's all I can do to keep up with the daily newspapers."

She started back to where she'd dropped her beach bag. Surprisingly, he followed, with Charlie bringing up the rear. "Look, if you're having second thoughts about associating with me," Jackson announced, "I wish you'd just come right out and say so. You don't have to worry that I'll force myself on you."

That was the least of her concerns! The only person she'd really punish by keeping her distance was herself, and hadn't some sage once decreed that half a loaf was better than none?

"*Are* you having second thoughts?" Jackson persisted.

She shook her head. "Not exactly. I just don't think we can make this 'friendship' business work."

But she was wrong, as the following days proved. They saw each other only on the beach and never by design, yet it was as though some prearranged signal drew them together there at the same time, whether it was dawn, high noon, or dusk. And, contrary to what Laura might have expected, they came to know each other.

To begin with, she mostly talked and he listened, something he did very well. But gradually he let drop little snippets of information about himself almost by accident.

One day, he made what amounted to a lengthy speech, for him. He noticed a ship, hull down on the horizon, and began in a faraway voice, "When I was a kid, I wanted to sail the seven seas and conquer the whole world."

Laura didn't reply; she barely breathed, in case he remembered she was there and lapsed into one of his familiar silences.

"When I outgrew that fantasy, I decided I wanted to fly a fighter jet." A faint grin touched his features. "But, by the time I was fourteen, I knew I was going to be too tall to fit in the cockpit. So then I settled for following in my uncle's footsteps. It seemed like a good plan—he'd been my boyhood hero from the time I was old enough to ride on his shoulders."

"Did you succeed?" she inquired, when the silence threatened to go on indefinitely.

"Hell, I hope not!"

His tone was so bitter that she couldn't help asking one more question. "Why, what happened?"

"He died, and so did my dreams. I grew up and learned that only gods belong on pedestals."

And then he pressed his lips together and stared distantly out to sea in a way she'd come to recognize. It meant that the subject of Jackson Connery was closed for the day and it was up to her to carry the conversational ball from there on.

When that happened, she'd rattle on about her own life. She told him about her partnership with Archie in the Sunderland Gallery, and the traveling it entailed throughout Europe and the Orient and South America to attend art auctions. And when she finally ran dry Jackson would say, in his deep, quiet voice, something like, "There's a hummingbird investigating the flowers on your beach towel. Don't move your foot, sweet face, or you'll scare him away."

Sometimes she wondered if he'd paid attention to anything she'd said, but then, later, he'd remark on some fact that would show that he'd not missed a word. She suspected that he couldn't, or wouldn't, allow himself to show too much interest in her revelations in case she got the wrong ideas about where their friendship might lead.

Along the same lines, he'd occasionally sit companionably by her side, but more often kept distance between them as though to be too close was to tempt the flesh too severely. He never fully lowered the barriers of privacy, even though she tried every subtle ruse she could come up with to elicit information from him. The last thing she ever expected was that he'd invite her to join him for dinner.

"I've got a pail full of clams, far more than even I can eat at one sitting," he told her one hot afternoon. "Do you want to come down after sunset when it's a bit cooler, and help me get rid of them? We could have a clambake on the beach."

It wasn't the most glamorous or the most gracious invitation she'd ever received, but it marked a milestone in the relationship. Laura couldn't recall ever being more excited about a date. "I'd love it," she said, steeling herself not to gush with sheer pleasure.

It was a fabulous night, all diamond stars against a black velvet sky, the way it was supposed to be in all the best love songs. The sand was still warm from the sun, and the ocean rustled and muttered like a well-fed baby settling down to sleep. Laura and Jackson stuffed themselves on clams and Wanda's sourdough bread. Jackson even produced a bottle of wine.

"I'll remember this place for as long as I live," he remarked, leaning back against a chunk of driftwood and exhaling deeply. "It will always be the place I began to find some peace again."

By then, Laura knew better than to ask what he meant by that. Better to pretend she hadn't given the comment all that much attention, and change the subject. "As a child, I spent every holiday here. Every summer—and in those days they were all hot and full of sunshine with never a drop of rain—and every Christmas too, when the shore would be edged with a frill of ice and Frank used to say the wind was enough to cut a grown man in half," she replied, hoping the revelation would persuade him to trade more childhood memories with her. "My recollections of those years are filled with memories of Carter's Cove. I sometimes think everything of significance happened to me here—growing up, learning about life..." *Falling in love*?

"Happy times," he said, rather wistfully, she thought.

"Sad times, too. I learned about death, the spring that I was ten and Taffy died. She was Honey Bee's golden retriever and I couldn't remember a time when she wasn't there, tail waving a welcome. We found her outside one morning, on the terrace next to the daffodils. Frank buried her under the dogwood tree, and I cried all day. That night, Honey Bee brought me out to the terrace again and showed me the star where she said all the dogs go after their time on earth is finished. She told me that Taffy was happy there with lots of new friends, and could look down and see where she used to live." Her voice wobbled dangerously. "And we have to change the subject right this minute, or I'll be crying again at the memory."

Jackson understood. "Sirius," he said gently, and pointed to the sky. "The Dog Star, see? It's the brightest star in the heavens, and I'm sure your Taffy's very happy there."

"How did you know where it is?"

He shrugged and looked out across the faint pearl sheen of the ocean. "Oh, I've spent a few nights star-gazing in my time, wishing I was out there with nothing but wide open space around me. Many's the time I'd have traded the company I was keeping for that I'd find on Sirius. There's a lot of truth in that saying 'The more I see of other people, the better I like my dog!'"

Laura thought of the people she knew. Archie and his wife, Molly. Friends, business associates. Good, decent people, every one. She thought about smiles from strangers she'd passed in the street, remembered a young man holding the elevator for her, not because she was a woman but because it was a considerate thing to do. And she wondered again what made

Jackson so bitter, and she couldn't help asking, "Why don't you like anyone?" even though, in doing so, she ran the risk of having him shut her out in that abrupt way of his.

This time, though, he surprised her by laughing. "I like a few. Your great-grandmother, for instance, and Wanda because she's a terrific cook—and even you, sometimes."

She wished she dared believe him, but, "You don't need any of us," she said sadly.

"No," he agreed. "I don't." Then, as though he knew she was about to argue the point, he went on, "None of us really needs another person, you know. We choose to let people into our lives when, in the final analysis, the only one we can absolutely count on is ourselves."

She couldn't let it go at that. "Have you never loved *anyone*, Jackson? Your parents, a brother or sister? Don't you have *any* friends who are important to you?"

"I was an only child and my parents are both dead. But to answer your questions, yes, I loved them. And yes, I have one or two friends who are important to me—but I don't *need* them. I don't rely on them or ask anything of them. I don't entrust them with my happiness, nor do I feel I have the right to inflict my misery on them."

Then they're not really your friends, Jackson, she thought, but knew that voicing such an opinion would damage the fragile intimacies she was sharing that night with a man who gave new meaning to the term "strong, silent type." No wonder he was so fond of clams!

One day during the third week of August he surprised her with another invitation. "The water's much warmer than it was a month ago," he said. "How about going skin-diving with me this afternoon?"

Oh, life was unfair sometimes! What she wouldn't have given to have their relationship progress to something beyond the stage of unplanned conversation that sometimes lasted less than half an hour. But skin-diving? "No," she replied firmly.

"Why not?"

She fiddled with the strap of her thongs, refusing to look him in the eye. "Because," she muttered.

"Because? That's no answer, Laura Mitchell, and you know it." Baffled, he inched closer and, taking her chin between his thumb and forefinger, turned her face to him. "Did I say something to upset you?"

"No."

"Then why won't you——?"

She sighed and admitted, "Because I'm not that fond of the water."

"But I've seen you swim."

"I manage to keep afloat," she corrected him, "but I'm not big on aquabatics."

At that, he laughed with genuine amusement. "*Aquabatics*, Laura?"

"You know what I mean. If God had intended me to be fooling about underwater, He'd have given me fins. If you must know, I'm afraid of the ocean and the only reason I go in at all is that I hate giving in to silly fears."

"It's not silly to be cautious with the ocean, sweet face," he said, sobering. "Only fools pretend otherwise."

"Nevertheless," she said stubbornly, "I'm not going skin-diving with you. The mere idea of having a rubber mask clamped to my face, then sticking my head underwater, terrifies me." She shuddered. "There are things down there."

"What sort of things?"

She took inventory of her limited knowledge. "Mud sharks and octopus."

"Octopi," he reminded her, "and they're extremely shy. Furthermore, it's unlikely you'd ever see one unless you were down at least thirty feet, which means you'd be scuba diving. You can stay on the surface to skin-dive."

"I don't have the proper equipment."

"I have a spare mask and snorkel which you're welcome to keep. Do yourself a favor and give it a try. You'll be amazed at what you'll see."

Still she hesitated. The temptation to share a new experience with him beckoned, but old fears weren't easily dismissed. "I don't know..."

"The water's pretty calm today and there are no undertows to worry about. In fact, the tide will have turned by this afternoon, so the worst that can happen is that you'll get washed ashore." He took her hand and squeezed her fingers reassuringly. "What's the matter, don't you trust me?"

"Only slightly more than I trust myself," she muttered, dismayed at how his touch and the warmth of his smile reduced her to a quivering mass of jelly inside. Hadn't repeated exposure granted her *any* immunity to him? "How far out will we have to go?"

Gauging the distance through narrowed eyes, he pointed to an embrasure in the rocks where the water glistened pale turquoise. "About halfway between the beach and the headland."

The desire to hoard memories of the time spent with him overrode caution. "Okay," she agreed, quickly, before she lost her nerve.

"Laura," he coaxed, several hours and two failed attempts later, "just breathe normally and don't panic."

The water flooded the snorkel, she couldn't breathe, she was drowning. Lifting her head, she tore off the mask, and gulped air into her lungs. "I can't——!"

"Yes, you can. There's nothing to it, once you get the hang of things."

Her nose felt raw from the saltwater she'd inhaled. "Ahh! That's easy...for you to say."

"Sweet face, you're floating on the surface." His hand under her ribs spelt safety, his voice reassured her. "Try again. Just submerge the mask enough for the water to cover it, and take a slow breath."

His other hand pressed softly against the back of her head, cajoling her into making one last try. "I'm right here beside you," he promised, his words a ribbon of security weaving around her.

She wanted to make him proud and hated herself for her cowardice. The incoming tide surged, retreated, rolled her high, then dropped her into a clear green valley. Somewhere below, barely out of sight, unimaginable predators waited. "There's nothing to see," she wailed.

He trod water so that he was facing her. Even behind the thick glass of the mask his eyes gleamed summer blue. "Once more," he wheedled, "and if you can't do it this time I won't insist."

Why should it matter that she not let him down in something so insignificant in the wider order of things? Yet matter it did. Terribly.

She pulled the mask into place, adjusted the snorkel, counted to ten.

"Slowly," he murmured, his voice as soothing as the lazy curl of a wave.

She lowered her face, felt the cool water lap around her head, and schooled herself to draw in a long, controlled breath. Miraculously, air filtered into her lungs. Around her, prisms of turquoise light flickered and danced from the brilliance of the afternoon above.

Suddenly, Jackson's face swam into view and even though half his features were hidden behind the mask she knew he was smiling. He gave her the universal thumbs-up sign of victory, then reached for her and pulled her with him in a slow and easy motion.

From the corner of her eye, she saw the dark ribs of the cliff sweeping down to the rippled sand of the sea floor. A slender shape flitted by, more timid than she. Overhead, the sun shone hot on her back, reminding her that the familiar world was literally no more than a hair's breadth away. Beside her, Jackson held her hand, anchoring her to safety. Suddenly, a flutter of shadows disturbed the calm, and she gazed in startled fascination as schools of small red and yellow striped fish darted into sight between strands of amber seaweed.

Jackson nudged her and gestured to the left. Beams of sunlight slanting through the water revealed huge purple starfish and illuminated the waving fronds of white and orange sea anemones. A vivid green fish that she didn't recognize kept a respectful distance from spiny sea urchins, while a sculpin peered out from his home under a rock, watching with bright, beady eyes as a hermit crab scurried by.

It was beautiful down there, an undersea garden full of silent, graceful life that she never would have discovered had it not been for Jackson.

"Well?" When they eventually surfaced, he shoved back his mask and hers, then spanned her waist with both hands and buoyed her up in the water. "Was it worth it?"

"Yes!" She gripped his shoulders for balance and, thoroughly delighted with herself, burst into spontaneous laughter. "It was wonderful! I felt like a mermaid! Aren't you proud of me?"

He rode the gentle swell of a wave, his eyes creased with laughter. "Yes, I'm proud of you, brat! Pity I can't treat *you* to raw herring as a reward."

High above, a bald eagle hovered against the cloudless sky and just for a moment life seemed quite perfect. Then the wave subsided, sweeping her and Jackson into the shade of the cliff, and suddenly the laughter disappeared along with the sun and she was drowning, not in the cool green water lapping around her waist, but in the scorching blue depths of his eyes.

## CHAPTER SIX

ONE of Jackson's hands loosened and slid up Laura's spine; the other flexed around her hips. She felt her breasts skimming the length of his chest, her thighs tangling with his. Her head was above water, yet the constriction in her lungs was more acute than anything she'd experienced with the snorkel. She was suffocating, drowning, dying—and it was agony, because his mouth hovered an eternity away, denying her access to heaven.

"Jackson," she begged on a frail breath.

His gaze settled on her lips contemplatively, memorized each curve, then drifted back to her eyes, casting such a potent spell along the way that she felt her lids closing with the weight of it. His head inched close enough that she could feel his lashes flutter along her cheek.

"Lorelei," he muttered in reply, and then, mere seconds before the torture destroyed her, his mouth claimed hers.

Time whirled, sending the sun spinning and churning the water around them. The desire she'd tried so hard to dispel rose up to meet the hunger in him. Her arms locked around his neck, her legs around his waist.

He was all muscled strength and hard, indomitable masculinity. She flung aside the knowledge that the most he was willing to offer her was friendship, and shut out the clamoring voice of conscience until it whimpered into silence. She called on every feminine wile at her disposal to seduce him into forgetting his most dearly held intentions, and immersed herself fully in the sensations that battered her, willing to barter life itself if that was the price she had to pay for this brief interlude of dazzling promise.

She combed her fingers through his hair, touched his mouth, sipped drops of water from his jaw. She swayed against his chest until she thought her nipples would leap free from the constraints of her swimsuit.

She heard Jackson groan deep in his chest, felt his hands searching, his body seeking, probing. The heat of him scorched her, imprinted itself against her, and only the taut fabric of her suit prevented him from making her completely his.

Then he touched her again, his palm cupping her with unbearable intimacy, his fingers slipping past the elasticized silk to find a smoother satin. And she shot to heights of sensation that were terrifying in their intensity. She heard a voice, husky with emotion, and knew it must be hers because his tongue was wreaking havoc with her breast. She felt a slow coiling of tension, braced herself for an assault that she was sure would shatter her, and wrenched his mouth up to seal hers in order to prevent herself from telling him over and over how much she wanted him to continue, how much she loved him. How much . . . how much . . .

Who knew where it all might have ended, if nature hadn't intervened? Not Laura. She was awash in passion so far outracing control that she'd stopped caring about anything as mundane as the tide. But the ocean chose that moment to assert its authority and put an end to a kiss that spiraled to the pit of her stomach. One minute she was clinging to Jackson with limpet determination, her mouth sealed to his, her hips brazenly inciting him to further trespass, and the next she was struggling to be free and fighting for breath as a wave dashed over her head.

It happened not a moment too soon. God help him, another minute and he would have taken her. The thin stuff of her swimsuit had abetted him without shame, slipping aside to allow him unlimited access to the cool cream flesh of her body that the sun never saw.

He'd watched her eyes grow heavy and dazed with passion, had deliberately tested his own powers of resistance beyond reason even though, for days, he'd been fighting a battle with a desire that paid not the slightest heed to anything reasonable. What the hell had he hoped to prove? That he was made of stone? Or that the experts had been right when they'd said no man emerged from his particular kind of hell with his integrity intact?

"Listen," he said, holding her firmly at arm's length when they both surfaced again, "I didn't mean for this to happen. You have to believe that."

"How can I," she asked, skewering him with the honesty of her green-eyed gaze, "when we both wanted it so much and know it felt so right?"

"It wasn't right!" he said, the torment raging inside. "It will never be right for us. If you can't accept that, then we might as well forget all this——" He stopped and ground his teeth in new frustration. Where were the words to tell her? How did a man kill something unbelievably beautiful and not lift a finger to stop the destruction?

He drew in a calming breath and tried again. "We might as well forget about friendship and go back to being adversaries, both sticking to our own patch of territory, because we'll end up enemies anyway."

Her face seemed to diminish until she was all eyes full of pain. He kicked away, practically shoving her underwater in his haste to put more distance between them before he fell victim to temptation again. He couldn't bear, didn't dare, to look at the soft, hurt mouth. Bad enough that he'd never forget the taste of it.

"Leave me alone," he begged wretchedly. "For God's sake, Lorelei, go away and forget this afternoon ever happened."

She did as he asked because he left her no choice. She was not so far gone that she'd throw herself at a man who obviously regretted his brief moment of wanting her. If, despite everything she did to make it behave otherwise, her body wanted him, it was not something she intended to advertise.

But she hurt. She hurt so much that she began to question how in control of her feelings she really was, because she had a growing suspicion she wasn't going to find it easy to shrug off Jackson Connery and chalk their so-called friendship up to experience.

She was tempted to cut short her holiday, but Honey Bee's distress at the mere mention of such a thing persuaded her otherwise. It wasn't an option she really cared for anyway. Not only was Carter's Cove the place she loved best on earth, she didn't like to think she'd become the sort of woman who ran away when things didn't turn out the way she wanted them to.

However, to avoid exacerbating the pain by running into Jackson all the time, she took to walking over the headland to the next bay. Much rockier than the other beach, it was neither as pretty nor as accessible, but it was sheltered.

If there was one good outcome to her relationship with Jackson, it was discovering the pleasures of skin-diving. The huge lagoons left behind at low tide were milk warm in the late August sun and the hours she spent floating idly on the surface, enjoying the sea life six feet below, offered soothing relief to her injured spirit.

One afternoon, she ventured out a little farther than usual to a shelf between two rocky points where the water was deeper. That was when she found the swimming scallops, a whole herd of them skipping along, propelled by the castanet action of their rosy, fluted shells.

Absorbed, she didn't notice that she'd floated into much shallower water until her foot became entangled in a large ribbon of dark seaweed. At that, all her repressed horror of lurking predators came flooding back and her only concern was to free herself as quickly as possible. Kicking wildly, she felt her foot make contact with the surface of a large chunk of rock covered with something rough and scaly. Before she had time to register the pain, one razor edge had sliced between her toes like a knife through butter, and suddenly the water around her was bright with blood.

She didn't have a whole lot of choice about what to do, once she was back on the beach. She was a good mile away from the house and any sort of help. Wincing as the sting of salt and grit made their presence felt in her wound, she set about fashioning a bandage from her towel. It was thick and clumsy, but it staunched the flow of blood and kept the cut reasonably free of dirt as she began the arduous climb up the cliff.

She slipped and she scrabbled, grabbing hold of roots and shrubs in an attempt to lever herself up without putting pressure on her injury. Try as she might, though, hopping just didn't work and by the time she finally reached the top she'd lost half her snorkeling gear, the towel bandage had come all untied, and her foot was throbbing. In fact, she felt so rotten that she sank down on the shady side of a salal bush and wished her guardian angel would appear and fly her back to Honey Bee's.

Jackson showed up instead. "What the hell——!" Catching sight of the bloody towel, he dropped everything he was carrying and came racing over to investigate. "What happened to you?"

"I was tap dancing and slipped," she snapped, pain and irritation getting the better of her. "What does it look like?"

"As though you were playing barefoot on oyster beds," he said, examining the cut, "which is ridiculous because you're much too smart to do anything that stupid." He glanced up, his gaze compelling. "Aren't you, Laura?"

"I'm not in the mood for a lecture, Jackson. Go home and leave me alone."

"Sure thing. That's just my style, leaving a woman to bleed to death on a lonely cliff."

All the time he talked, he was poking at her foot, moving her baby toe back and forth as though to be sure it was still firmly attached. "That hurts," she said plaintively.

"I can't imagine why," he said dryly. "It's only sliced clean to the bone. Can you stand up?"

"On one leg."

He held out both hands. "That's good enough. Grab a hold."

"Ouch!" But the pain hardly had time to register before he'd hauled upright and hoisted her over his shoulder. With her face dangling halfway down his back and her nose bobbing against his spine, he set off, tramping along the path as though she weighed no more than a child.

"You want me to carry you up to the house?" he asked.

"Like this?"

"How else?"

In his arms would have been nice. She could have suffered the pain in her foot a lot more easily with her head resting romantically against his shoulder. "Well, this isn't very comfortable," she told him.

But romance was clearly the furthest thing from his mind. "It beats limping along on one good leg." He gave her a heave and settled his arm more firmly across the backs of her knees. "I hope Frank can drive you to the clinic in town. You're going to need stitches and possibly a tetanus shot."

"Sorry to disappoint you, Jackson, but Frank's taken the Jeep into Potter's Landing for servicing, and Honey Bee doesn't have a driver's license any longer."

Jackson muttered something short and unflattering under his breath. "Then I suppose I'll have to take you in myself."

For a knight in shining armor, he was not exactly gracious. "It might surprise you to learn," Laura said between clenched teeth, as he hit an uneven section on the trail and jarred her foot unpleasantly, "that I didn't do this on purpose to spoil your day."

"Sweet face," he replied on a sigh, "you've been spoiling my days—and my nights, come to that—for so long now that I'm becoming used to it."

She digested that in pleased silence for a while, and a tiny hope flickered to life. It faded rather quickly, though, as he traversed another rough spot and a more immediate concern struck her. "I hope you're not planning to cover the fifteen miles of back road into Pearce with me traveling upside down like this because, if you are, I think I'd just as soon not bother."

"We'll go in on the bike."

Surprise piqued her curiosity, temporarily eclipsing the pain in her foot. "What bike?"

They were approaching the cabin. "Mine," he said, preparing to lower her onto the porch. "Try not to put any weight on your foot and just sit here on the steps while I find a better bandage."

"I didn't know you had a bike," she said.

"How did you think I got supplies out here? By carrier pigeon?"

"I didn't think about it at all. Where do you keep it—the bike, I mean?"

"Under a tarp at the side of the porch. Don't tell me you didn't notice it on your little spying mission?"

Throughout their verbal sparring, he'd been busy inside the cabin. When he came out again, he carried a bowl of water that smelled strongly of disinfectant, and a first-aid kit. "This isn't a pretty sight," he said, kneeling in front of her and swabbing away the dirt and blood on her foot. "Perhaps it's just as well your great-grandmother won't know anything about it until it's been properly taken care of." He looked up, his eyes dark with concern. "How are you feeling?"

"Rather cold." In fact, she was shivering.

"Shock," he pronounced. "Pity you don't have anything warmer to wear than what you've got on, but I've got a sweater that'll cover you up a bit."

He made a pad out of gauze, then proceeded to bandage her foot with admirable skill. "You're very good at this," Laura observed. "Are you sure you're not really a doctor in disguise?"

"Quite sure," he said shortly. "Does your foot hurt much?"

"Not really. Actually, it's quite numb."

"That won't last," he predicted. "It's going to get jarred on the ride in and you won't feel like tap dancing by the time we get there, I can assure you."

She must indeed be in shock because her only thought at that moment was that it would be worth all the discomfort and inconvenience just to spend the next couple of hours close to him. And it was—at first.

"Wrap your arms around my waist and hang on tight, sweet face," he said. "This is going to be a bumpy trip."

They took off in a spurt of gravel. She snuggled down inside the heavy fisherman's knit sweater he'd given her, and sheltered behind his wide, capable shoulders. But, even though he tried to avoid the worst potholes, every time they hit a bump on the track the pain shot from her foot up into her leg, and by the time they arrived at the clinic she felt sick to her stomach.

Jackson must have noticed. He didn't say anything, but he sat close beside her in the waiting room and twined his fingers around hers.

She wasn't prepared for the reaction that stole over her. She looked at his broad, sun-brown hands, at his strong, beautiful profile, and her heart turned over. This was how it was always meant to be between them, she thought, certainty rising up to choke her. He might not always be reasonable or easy to get along with, but a woman would know she could trust her life to a man like him.

Yet it seemed that she was not to be that woman, and all at once she couldn't bear it. The tears flooded her eyes without warning and before she could turn away they were splashing over the back of his hand.

"Hey, what's all this?" Jackson asked softly. "The pain?"

She shook her head, unable to speak.

"What, then?" Reaching for a box of tissues on the table beside him, he pulled out a handful and mopped awkwardly at her face. "Are you afraid of needles as well as the ocean, sweet face? Is that it?"

She gulped. "Oh, Jackson . . .!"

"I'll be right here with you the whole time and you can squeeze my hand until I yell for mercy, if you like. I'm probably a bigger coward than you. Men aren't nearly as tough as women, you know. That's why we aren't the ones who give birth."

I'd give birth to a dozen strapping sons without a murmur if you were willing to father them and stay by me for the rest of my life, she almost told him, and decided that she must be in worse shape than she realized to allow such a wildly improbable idea to cross her mind.

"Is that why you won't let yourself fall in love? Because you're afraid?" she asked instead.

He didn't answer, nor did he move, not even to disengage his hand. He simply froze, and she was reminded of the time she'd spent a weekend with friends who owned a horse ranch in the country. She'd visited the stables to see their prize stallion, a magnificent black creature whose utter stillness was a warning in itself not to presume too far on its tameness. The same half-wild aura settled on Jackson now, and she had only herself to blame.

"I don't know why I asked that," she muttered. "It isn't any of my business, nor is it why I was crying."

"So what was the reason?" he finally asked.

"Oh..." She floundered, searching for a plausible explanation for being such an emotional fool. "I wanted to catch some swimming scallops and take them home to Honey Bee——"

"What?" A muffled explosion of laughter escaped him.

"Yes," Laura babbled. "She loves them, and I was so thrilled to discover them—I'd had a lovely afternoon, you see, until things started going wrong and..." Oh, Lord, she was going to start crying again unless something happened to distract her! She raked back her hair, which was stiff with salt, and swiped at the damp tracks left by her tears. "I feel rotten and must look a mess."

"You do," he agreed with faint amusement, "but that's understandable, given the circumstances."

Fortunately, she was called into the treatment room just then. When she joined Jackson half an hour later, with her foot all sutured and bandaged, she had regained control of herself and was able to smile, albeit wanly. "All done," she declared. "I have to make an appointment for next Tuesday afternoon when the stitches come out, then we can leave."

Dusk had fallen and the air was sweet with the scent of late summer. Although the stars were out, the sky possessed a luminous afterglow against which the trees cast black silhouettes. During the ride home, Laura pressed herself against Jackson's spine, imprinting the shape and texture of him on her memory because she knew with more certainty than ever that memories would be all she'd have with which to sustain herself during the long winter ahead.

But she would survive, she told herself. She would go back to the wonderful life she'd left behind, assume the old image of understated elegance clothed in success that was her trademark, and no one need ever guess that it was all a masquerade. Given enough time, surely she would eventually forget that she'd almost had her heart broken by a passing summer fancy?

Her foot healed well, and much faster than her wounded emotions, as she realized the following Tuesday. Wanda served swimming scallops for dinner and, noticing Laura's surprise, explained that Jackson had stopped by with them that afternoon.

"Such a kind and considerate man," Honey Bee beamed.

Gun-shy was a better description, Laura thought, staring resentfully at the delicate morsels on her plate. Not once while she'd been laid up had Jackson bothered to visit or inquire after her health. He knew very well that this was the day she had to go into Pearce to have her stitches removed, and had no doubt timed his visit to coincide with her absence. But Honey Bee was eyeing her with birdlike curiosity, so she agreed in her most noncommittal tones that Mr.

Connery certainly paid attention to a great many things.

Later that evening, Honey Bee brought up his name again. "Am I right in assuming you and Mr. Connery have overcome your differences, my love?"

"Mmm . . . hmm." Laura chewed the end of her pencil and frowned at the crossword puzzle in front of her, hoping her show of concentration would discourage further conversation on the subject of Jackson.

"Good, because he's coming for dinner on Saturday night."

Just briefly, Laura's composure cracked. "Saturday night?" she echoed, her voice shooting up half an octave. Then, noticing Honey Bee's renewed scrutiny, she collected herself and went on with feigned indifference, "Really? I didn't realize you'd spoken to him recently."

"Oh, yes! Didn't I mention it?" Honey Bee smoothed her needlepoint and surveyed it critically. "I happened to stop by the kitchen while he was here this afternoon, and we had a cozy little chat."

"No, you didn't mention it," Laura replied rather acidly. Somehow, the idea of Jackson and her great-grandmother enjoying a cozy little chat struck a false note. Neither of them was the cozy, chatty type, and Laura didn't like it any more than she liked the fact that Honey Bee couldn't quite look her in the eye. "So you invited him to dinner and he accepted without an argument? I confess I'm surprised."

"Ah, well, this time I refused to take no for an answer, and he's much too chivalrous to deny an old lady such a simple favor." Honey Bee did look up then, and impaled Laura with a very direct glance.

"Are you sure you don't mind my having invited him, my love?"

"Whatever makes you ask? I don't mind in the slightest." Laura traded stare for stare, and attempted a laugh that sounded horribly like Rose's Tinkerbell affectation. Sobering, she said, "What's a nine-letter word for 'self-deceptions,' third letter L?"

"Delusions," Honey Bee replied crushingly, "and I'm surprised you weren't able to come up with that solution yourself, Laura, all things considered."

It seemed wiser not to ask what that remark meant.

Honey Bee liked people to feel welcome when they stayed with her. Sleep late, retire early, eat when you're hungry and don't ask permission to raid the refrigerator was her motto. But one thing was clearly understood: everyone dressed for dinner. Nothing formal like black tie and evening gowns except for very special occasions, but shorts and T-shirts would have been an affront.

It was a custom that Laura always enjoyed. Gathering around Honey Bee's gracious dinner table was a lovely way to round off the day, winter or summer. And that, she reasoned, was why she took such trouble with her appearance on Saturday night.

Her full black skirt hugged her waist and flared out to swirl around her ankles. Her ivory silk blouse, cut so that not a crease or wrinkle marred its smooth perfection, dipped discreetly to show off her long, elegant neck and slender shoulders—probably the best feature in her unremarkable body, she decided—while not drawing attention to her "skinny endowments."

The sun had kindly renewed her tan and streaked her hair with highlights whose gleam almost matched the gold hoops in her ears and around her wrist. With the ease of long practice, she took only a moment to feather subtle jade shadow over her eyelids and sweep mascara over her lashes, so that people who didn't know better might be fooled into thinking she had greener eyes and longer lashes than those with which nature had, in fact, endowed her. A clever touch of blusher in just the right spots completed the make-over, adding hollows under her cheekbones that Sophia Loren would have applauded.

The grandfather clock on the landing struck a quarter past seven just as she sprayed Paloma Picasso's beguiling fragrance behind her ears and at her throat. She was as ready as she'd ever be to face Jackson across the table and make bright, inconsequential dinner conversation.

## CHAPTER SEVEN

JACKSON arrived promptly at seven-thirty, and the first thing Laura noticed about him was that he'd had his hair cut. Instead of straggling down the back of his neck, it barely brushed the collar of his shirt—the same white shirt, newly laundered and ironed, that he'd worn the first time he'd visited the house. His pants, though, she'd never seen before. Slim-fitting as only the Europeans could design them, they surely must have been tailored especially for him, so perfectly did they fit.

His gold-rimmed glasses peeped out of his breast pocket, and he was wearing a watch. She couldn't quite believe the latter. Somehow, he didn't seem like the sort of man who'd let himself be ruled by time.

He had shaved. He smelled not of after-shave, exactly, but of something light and pleasant. Pink soap and deep, clean well water, freshly drawn. He looked so powerfully beautiful that she didn't know how she was going to get through the evening without melting.

"Ahem!" Honey Bee's delicate cough alerted Laura to the fact that she'd been staring for far too long without speaking a word.

She swallowed and prayed that when she opened her mouth something appropriate and sophisticated would emerge. "Hello, Jackson," she croaked.

Honey Bee, who seemed on the verge of laughter, rescued her. "Mr. Connery, will you pour the drinks?"

"I'd be delighted to, Mrs. Carter, if you'll call me Jackson."

"I'd like sherry, Jackson, but there's Scotch or vodka if you prefer something a little stronger. Bring the tray out to the patio when you're ready. It's too lovely an evening to sit inside."

"Laura?" For the first time, he spoke directly to her.

The whole bottle of vodka with a straw seemed like a good idea, except that the stuff tasted like lighter fluid and she couldn't abide it. Furthermore, Jackson's presence incapacitated her faculties quite enough without an overdose of alcohol to add to her problems. "Sherry, please."

He busied himself with the paraphernalia of glasses and decanters, leaving Laura free to feast her eyes once more on the spread of his shoulders under the snowy shirt. Ice clinked against crystal. Her gaze slid past his collar and she knew an outrageous longing to press her lips to the nape of his neck, to taste his skin and fill her senses with the sun-fresh warmth of him.

"You're blocking the doorway."

Horrified, she realized he'd turned, tray in hand, and was watching her, seeming to read from her expression the turmoil she felt inside. She could only mumble an apology and hope that she was mistaken, that her thoughts hadn't paraded across her face with the same clarity that they'd invaded her mind.

If they had, he showed not the slightest interest in acknowledging them, and bent his attention on Honey Bee to such an extent that Laura might as well not have been there at all. Apart from a dutiful inquiry about her foot, he practically ignored her. The conversation flowed around her, both participants so engrossed in everything from animal rights to tax shelters that Laura was able to examine him again at her leisure without fear of provoking comment.

If she'd been asked, she'd have predicted that Jackson would be a taciturn and reluctant guest. The fragile-stemmed crystal ought to have looked ludicrous in his hands; he ought to have been drinking beer straight from the bottle. But, once again, he defied her expectations, handling himself and the situation with consummate grace. Honey Bee was clearly more charmed than ever.

Why am I surprised? Laura wondered, eyeing him over the rim of her wineglass as Wanda cleared away the main course. Not once in all the time she'd known him had he ever done the expected. Nor did he seem about to change his ways.

"What's the matter?" he murmured, leaning toward her. "Did you think I'd embarrass you by slurping my soup, or eating peas from my knife?"

She fixed her gaze on her plate. "I don't know what you're talking about."

"Liar," he mocked softly. "You're as amazed as if you'd found yourself sitting down to dinner with a well-trained ape."

"Are you suggesting I'm a snob?"

"No, sweet face." He smiled lazily, more relaxed than she'd ever seen him. "Just a little class conscious, which is what I've been trying to tell you all along."

Warmth stained her cheeks, less at the reproach than at the endearment. He didn't mean it literally, she knew, but when he said "sweet face" like that, sliding the words out of his mouth like a caress, it left her quivering inside.

If Honey Bee overheard their exchange, she didn't comment, but her eyes rested thoughtfully first on Jackson, then on Laura, in a way that made Laura distinctly uneasy. Rose's intuition paled beside Honey Bee's perspicacity when it came to making astute observations, and Laura feared she'd given away far too much of what she was feeling. She wished the evening would come to an end.

Her great-grandmother, however, did not seem disposed to make an early night of it. "Do you smoke, Jackson?" she asked, leading the way back outside after dinner and settling herself in one of the wicker patio chairs. Fat pillar candles flickered in glass hurricane lamps and cast a soft nimbus of light over the scene. To one side, Wanda had left coffee and brandy ready to be served from a brass tea trolley.

Jackson shook his head and sent an oblique glance Laura's way. "Not any more, Mrs. Carter. I was persuaded to give up such a filthy habit."

Honey Bee smiled. "Then what about music? Do you care for it?"

"Yes, ma'am, I do. It's saved my sanity on a number of occasions."

Why doesn't he ever confide in me like that? Laura wondered gloomily, as she poured the coffee. Honey Bee had wormed more out of him in two hours than she had managed in well over a month.

"I've got quite a collection of old favorites," Honey Bee told him. "They go all the way back to the thirties, some of them. Of course, the originals can't be played on modern stereo equipment, but I've been able to find duplicates on those wonderful compact discs they make nowadays. Take a look through them, Jackson, and put on something you'd like to hear. I think we've all had enough Mozart for one evening."

"Grandmother," Laura began, the moment he disappeared inside the house, "if you don't mind, I'm going to slip upstairs and leave you two alone. I'm——"

"Rubbish, my love," Honey Bee replied calmly. "You're going to do no such thing. Not only would it be extremely rude to our guest but, if anyone's going to slip away, it will be me. My age allows me that privilege. Yours, fortunately, does not."

"Stardust" filtered through the night, smooth and seductive. The candle flames swayed to the rhythm and flung their reflection on the lens of Jackson's glasses as he came back outside.

"An excellent choice." Honey Bee nodded approvingly. "My husband and I danced on this very patio to this particular number when it first came out—long before your time, of course."

"Yes." Jackson's voice was gentle. Removing his glasses, he propped them on the table. "I probably don't dance nearly as well as your husband, Mrs. Carter, but I would be very honored if you'd dance with me tonight."

She's eighty-nine years old, Laura wanted to protest. Her bones are fragile. She could fall and break a hip, and then what good will all your charm and chivalry do her?

But Honey Bee had taken his hand and was gliding in his arms with all the grace of a woman half her age. And he, so much taller, so much broader, held her protectively as they circled the slate paving stones of the patio. The candlelight drew fire from the diamonds on Honey Bee's fingers, and turned Jackson's hair the color of antique gold.

Laura's eyes filled with the tears that never seemed too far from the surface these days, and the ache that had started the day she first saw him on the beach intensified to such a pitch that she could barely draw breath. The empty corners of her life that she hadn't quite known what to do with—those rare, infrequent times when she'd look around in a group and know the special someone that God had created just for her wasn't a part of it—all made perfect sense, and she was tired of pretending otherwise.

She wanted Jackson to hold *her* protectively. She wanted his eyes to smile down at *her*, the way they smiled at Honey Bee. And the reason was simple: she'd found her special someone in him. She'd tried to resist him almost as hard as he'd managed to resist her, but she didn't have the stamina. The simple fact remained that she'd been bowled over by the feelings he aroused in her. She was in love with him, and had been almost from the beginning.

Ashamed and appalled, she turned in her chair and stared out at the darkened garden, away from the couple sharing this special moment. Things had come to a pretty pass indeed when she found herself jealous of the attention he was giving her eighty-nine-year-old great-grandmother.

A touch on her shoulder made her jump. "Dance with me," Jackson said.

"I can't," she replied stiffly. "I hurt my foot, remember?"

"Your foot's better. You're not even limping."

"I've had a sudden relapse. It's a miracle I'm not hobbling."

He leaned down and whispered against her ear, "The only miracle around here is that you don't have the longest nose in North America. You're lying again, sweet face."

"Only slightly. I absolutely will not dance with you."

"Yes, you will, because I promise not to step on your dainty toes." He took her hand and drew her to her feet, forestalling any further objections. "But most of all you'll do it because your great-grandmother would like to see you enjoying yourself instead of sitting in the corner like a sulky little girl."

A glance showed Honey Bee fanning herself and smiling across at her encouragingly. "Then I suppose I have no choice," Laura sighed, hating the ungraciousness she couldn't stem almost as much as she hated him at that moment.

This is how it would be to grow old and disappointed in love, she thought. Acid-tongued and bitter. The sort of relative that nephews had to be bribed to dance with at family parties. Except in her case, of course, she'd be spared that particular indignity, since she was nobody's aunt.

She held herself stiffly in Jackson's arms, even though the music had changed and "Slow Boat to China" cajoled her with its melody. He hooked one arm around the dip of her waist, pressed his palm to the small of her back and drew her snugly against him, thigh to thigh. The fingers of his other hand linked loosely with hers. A lone trumpet soared and Jackson's pulse beat against hers, two rhythms outracing each other.

Was it the moonlight, the whisper of the ocean, the music evoking nostalgia for an era when love was less complicated, that made him seem the epitome of everything romantic? He towered over her, dashing as Errol Flynn, suave as Cary Grant. Tall, handsome, mysterious. And so sexy, his effect on her was downright embarrassing.

Dear Lord, she thought helplessly, only love on a grand scale could be this terrifying up close!

Jackson watched her, catching every nuance of expression on her face. She felt again the searing intensity of his regard penetrate to the trembling heart of her. She could hide nothing from him but he, as usual, remained full of secrets. Almost.

His lashes lengthened into shadows that crept down his cheek. His mouth was unsmiling, almost angry, as if he raged against the desire that betrayed him where the cradle of his hips embraced her. And in his gaze...such depths, such torment, such...

"Close your eyes," he whispered and, pulling her closer, rested his chin on the crown of her head. She felt the resilience of grass beneath her feet and knew that he had maneuvered her beyond the aura of candlelight. She kicked off her high-heeled pumps, sank against him, and forgot that Honey Bee might be watching with wise and knowing eyes.

One melody slipped into another, hauntingly sweet: "Smoke Gets in Your Eyes," "Red Sails in the Sunset," "Harbour Lights." They knew what they were doing, those old composers. They understood love better than she ever would.

Jackson led her with gentle pressure at her hip and, even though he was so much taller, they danced as if they'd practiced together for years. For once, there was no conflict, no misunderstanding, no holding back. They were in perfect accord, even their hearts in tune. Bathed in moonglow, Laura had nothing but the cool grass beneath her feet and the moody wail of a clarinet to anchor her to earth.

She knew he was going to kiss her. That special electricity surging between them precluded any other outcome. His hand slid up her spine to cup the side of her neck. She raised her head and, through eyes grown heavy with desire, saw his mouth hover briefly before it came down to meet hers.

The music seemed to swell around them from a distance, sweeping them both into another dimension, one of holy silence where consequences, like reality, could not follow. The way he kissed her, there under the dappled shade of the old dogwood trees that bordered the lawn, made her feel as if he'd taken her soul very gently between his two strong hands and held it up to the sun. A fine, golden warmth shimmered through her, seeking out wells of passion she'd never before dared tap. "You Made Me Love You," a mellow saxophone foretold, and she knew nothing would ever be quite the same for her again.

His breath ruffled her lashes, traced a path from her temple to the lobe of her ear. The tremor that shook him communicated itself to her and, as though they were both afraid the other might fall, they locked their arms around each other. His lips reconnoitered her ear, a devastating kiss cloaked in an innocence she found terrifying for the scorching arousal it evoked.

Laura could not hold herself upright, could not command a single muscle of her body to obey her. She heard a small sound—her voice trapped in her throat, betraying her need with a whimper of protest that changed to a purr as he transferred attention to the corner of her mouth.

Her lips slackened, wanton as the rest of her. They parted and invited him to take whatever she had to offer that he found desirable. The warmth of him, the taste of him, flooded her. She was melting from every pore.

Then, suddenly, he lifted his head. "Listen," he whispered.

"What?" She sought his mouth again blindly. "I don't hear a thing."

"Exactly." His response feathered softly over her upturned face. "The music's stopped."

She heard her own voice, hollow with need. "But must we?"

A sigh rippled over him. "I'm many things, most of them reprehensible, no doubt, but taking advantage of my hostess's hospitality by seducing her great-granddaughter in the bushes offends even my tarnished sense of decency, Laura."

She wished she could resent him for blunting the magic of the moment with scruples. She wished she could subdue the urgent throb that swam the length of her to stain her cheeks pink. She wished he weren't so damned *right*.

"Honey Bee's gone inside," she said, drawing in a reviving breath of flower-drenched night air.

"Nevertheless——"

She turned away. "And so should I."

"Laura." He touched her elbow, almost apologetically. "The timing just isn't right."

"Was it ever?" she asked bitterly.

He brought his other hand up to her cheek. "Maybe, a long time ago."

Suddenly, all the pieces fell into place. She backed away from him, dismayed. "You're married. That's it, isn't it?"

"Hell, no!" Jackson laughed mirthlessly. "Nothing that simple."

Before this summer, she'd had no patience with women who got themselves involved with married men then cried about their broken hearts. Self-destructive behavior like that had made no sense to her. She supposed that, if she'd thought about it at all, she'd equated falling in love with bidding at an auction on a desirable work of art. It was an established fact that someone else might raise the stakes beyond one's capability to pay and, if that happened, the only smart thing to do was concede defeat and redirect one's energies elsewhere.

Now, she couldn't begin to imagine anything more devastating than falling in love with a man who belonged, legally and emotionally, to another woman. Relief that she'd been spared at least that much pain had her turning a deaf ear on the voice of reason that had been the lodestar of her adult years. Retracing her steps, she cupped his face in her hands.

"It's that simple for me," she said softly. "It's the only thing that could possibly make a difference to how I feel about you."

"Laura——!"

She saw the conflict in his eyes, hope and disbelief at war with each other, and she understood. Falling in love wasn't something she'd expected either, but after tonight—the way he'd kissed her, the way she'd responded not just with her body, but with her whole heart and soul—what choice had either of them but to confront their true feelings? They just needed time alone, that was all, to come to terms with the shock, and to savor the wonder of the miracle that had crept up when they weren't even looking.

"It's okay." Pulling his head down, she kissed him swiftly then released him. "I understand. I'm caught a little off-guard myself."

He turned towards the path that led to the beach steps. "Thank your great-grandmother for me. I'd have done it myself if I hadn't been too distracted to notice her go inside."

"I know." She nodded. "Good night, Jackson."

He stopped briefly, as though, decency and good manners notwithstanding, he couldn't bring himself to leave, then, "Yes," he said and, without giving temptation another chance to gain a foothold, he took off into the darkness.

It didn't matter. There was a lifetime of tomorrows waiting, and she wanted to share each one with him. She could afford to be generous with tonight.

Laura slept like a child. Awoke like one, too. Sweetly, with her heart light and full of anticipation. The sun shone. Birds sang. The sea was blue, blue as Jackson's eyes.

"Well, my love," Honey Bee observed, when she joined her great-grandmother in the solarium where they'd been taking breakfast during the heat wave, "my little dinner party wasn't so onerous after all, I take it?"

"It was very nice," Laura said demurely, then gave everything away with a smile that wouldn't have fooled a child. "In fact, it was the best idea you've ever had."

"Am I to assume from that that Jackson found the evening quite splendid, too?"

"I'm sure he did. In fact, he made a point of asking me to thank you. He'd have told you himself but he didn't notice you leave."

"I doubt either of you would have noticed an earthquake," Honey Bee remarked dryly. "Try this peach ginger preserve with your brioche, my love. It's Wanda's own recipe and also quite splendid in its way."

Laura felt her smile grow. "You knew before I did how I felt, didn't you?"

Honey Bee seldom dissembled, even with questions as vague as this. "I tend to be suspicious of unfounded hostility between a man and a woman," she said. "It's almost always based on something other than antipathy."

"I'm almost ready to believe in miracles." Laura spread her hands, palms up. "Does that make me hopelessly naive?"

"Not at all." Honey Bee paused delicately. "What about Jackson? Does he feel the same way?"

Laura clasped her hands together, one fist clenched inside the other. "Oh, I hope so! I think so."

But, during the course of the day, she began to wonder. Not quite sure exactly what she'd expected next, she knew only a sense of anticipation that gradually turned into apprehension as the hours rolled by and nothing happened. He didn't come to call. He wasn't to be found on the beach.

After lunch, she went for a walk past his cabin, but it was deserted except for Charlie snoozing in the shade of the porch. She concluded that perhaps Jackson had gone into Pearce on some errand and that was why he hadn't yet contacted her.

Back at the house, she roamed restlessly. The afternoon droned past, its humidity and heat sapping her energy as well as her spirits.

With her customary tact, Honey Bee refrained from comment. "If you don't mind, my love," was all she said as the dinner hour approached, "I think I'll take a light supper in my room. I find this heat quite enervating."

Alone with nothing to distract her, Laura found it near impossible to keep her growing uncertainty under control. If, as seemed likely, Jackson was going to let the day go by without getting in touch, what was she supposed to infer? That she'd taken his response to her last night and blown it out of all proportion? That what had been a momentous self-discovery for her had been of no consequence whatsoever to him?

It occurred to her then that she was displaying all the symptoms of unrequited love that she'd pitied in other women of her acquaintance—hanging around, waiting for a doorbell that didn't ring, and staking her future happiness on the whim of a glance, a word.

She'd often wondered how people could allow themselves to fall victim to such misery. Well, now she knew. When the heart subjugated reason, a person wasn't left with too many other options.

"I'm not terribly hungry," she said, when Wanda came to announce dinner.

The housekeeper looked concerned. "You're not ill, I hope?"

Only if lovesickness qualified as a disease! "Not exactly. It's just the heat, I suppose. It's taken the edge off my appetite."

"I made cold salmon with a cucumber salad," Wanda said sympathetically, "but if there's something else you fancy...?"

What she fancied, Laura thought wryly, was a valid excuse to go banging on Jackson's door, a reason that would provide her with the chance to see him again without her pride being dragged through the dust.

Fishing in the pocket of her apron, Wanda unwittingly gave her just that. "Oh, by the way, the gentleman left these behind last night." She held out Jackson's gold-rimmed glasses. "I found them on the patio table this morning and meant to mention them sooner, but I forgot. I hope he hasn't been wondering where he left them."

Talk about a gift from the gods! "Don't worry about it," Laura said, her appetite suddenly improving. "I'll take a stroll over to his place a bit later on and return them myself. And maybe I will have a little of that salmon after all."

## CHAPTER EIGHT

LAURA waited until the sun sat low on the horizon before she set out. She'd changed into a lemon cotton sundress printed with forget-me-nots and big white daisies. It had a full skirt and a fitted bodice held up by spaghetti-straps, and was pretty enough to boost her confidence without making her feel overdressed for the occasion.

This time Jackson was home. The soft plucking of a guitar floated up from the hollow to meet her on her approach from the bluff, and all the anxiety she'd suffered during the day, all the doubts and uncertainties, disappeared like puffs of mist in a breeze as she recognized the tune.

He sat on the top step of the porch, head bent, spine supported by one of the posts holding up the roof. A six-string guitar rested easily across his thighs. His fingers, long and supple, coaxed forth the melody that had echoed through her memory all day: "You Made Me Love You."

Enthralled, she stopped in the shadow of a fir tree on the slope just behind him. Wearing a pale blue T-shirt and jeans, he looked so much at one with his surroundings that it seemed sacrilegious to intrude.

Within seconds, though, his fingers slowed and the last note faded into the dusk. He neither turned nor moved toward her; he merely stared out across the plum-colored ocean and said, "I somehow knew that you wouldn't have the good sense to stay away and leave well enough alone."

Experience ought to have taught her the futility of trying to sneak up on him undetected. From the beginning, she'd noticed that he possessed an uncanny talent for sensing another's presence, much like a wild animal whose instincts for self-preservation were on permanent alert. And it shouldn't have surprised her at all that he'd fight his attraction to her. He wasn't a man who'd be easily captured or tamed.

She covered the last few yards to the foot of the steps and confronted him. "Would you like me to leave?"

"Would it make any difference if I did?" he asked, resignation manifest in his tone.

For a moment she didn't reply. Instead, she gazed at him quite steadily and, for the first time, outstared him. His glance faltered, then swung past her to fix itself on the darkening sky, and she knew that her heart had not played her for a fool, after all. The realization lent her amazing courage.

"Do you think," she inquired softly, "that if you rebuff me now it will make me forget how you kissed me last night? Or do you really believe, Jackson, that I am such an innocent that I don't know how a man's desire betrays him?"

She advanced a step nearer and pressed a forefinger to the pulse beating savagely at his throat. "You couldn't have slipped a sheet of tissue paper between us when we danced last night, we held each other so close. I know how much you wanted me, Jackson..." She closed the remaining distance separating them, let her breath feather over him. "But do you have any idea how much I wanted you?"

He propped the guitar against the weathered railing. His hands, she noticed, were trembling. "You're about as knowledgeable as a newborn babe, at least where I'm concerned," he said roughly. "You don't know enough to realize you're playing with fire—or that flaunting your sweet young body before a man like me is the same as sticking your bare hand into a furnace."

She stroked a finger over his mouth to soften his anger. "Perhaps not, but there's more involved here than just sex."

He flinched away from her touch. "You're a walking innocent with no road sense. Hell, you've got no sense, period."

"Sense has nothing to do with what's happening between us, any more than——"

"Listen to me!"

"Listen to *me*!" she said and, reaching for his hand, pressed it to her rib cage so that he could feel the furious beat of her heart. "Listen to what really matters, Jackson."

She saw his eyes darken. His face was that of a man in torment, its beautiful planes sculpted with a wanting that undermined anything he could devise in the way of objection. The tips of his fingers stole unwillingly up the curve of her breast to trace the circumference of her nipple with unbearable tenderness.

She couldn't help herself. She covered his hand with hers and pressed herself into his palm because she thought it would ease the aching. But all it did was heighten her desire and snap his control in half.

A sound escaped her, not a cry, not a sigh, but something in between. The deeper echo of his voice murmured a response that was almost a groan, as though Atlas had decided the world was too heavy for one pair of shoulders and had chosen Jackson's to help share the load.

She lowered her face to his hair, filled herself with the smell and texture of it. "I love you," she mouthed in whispers too frail for him to decipher.

But, as though she'd shouted the words out loud, he responded. His other hand cupped itself lovingly around the back of her knee and, just as he had explored her breast, with precise and measured reluctance, so he discovered her thigh, inch by trembling inch.

Shock and pleasure combined to steal her breath away. No man had ever touched her like that, with such delicate, deliberate intent. Sensation coursed through her, more intense than that she'd experienced the day Jackson had taken her snorkeling. Then, events had conspired without warning, leaving her unprepared for what might happen next.

But this—oh, this was different. This was planned seduction—her plan, her seduction. He'd called her Lorelei, and she'd waited until now to live up to the name. She'd come here after the bright, revealing light of high summer had softened into dusk, determined that, this time, there would be no interruptions, no holding back. She'd thought she was in control. What a naive creature she was!

Slowly, Jackson rose. Trailing his hand hypnotically over the curve of her hip, he drew the skirt of her dress up around her waist then hauled her abruptly to him so that her hips nestled against his.

"How badly do you want me?" he whispered, his mouth nudging at hers until her lips parted. Then he kissed her, a sly, devastating kiss that begged the question.

She wanted him with a hot and aching urgency hitherto unknown to her. It sapped the strength from her limbs and pooled heavily where the evidence of his own arousal surged against her. It left her gasping and brought tears dancing to her eyes. It had her mouth softening, accommodating, offering. Promising everything she had to give without regard for what she might receive in return. She was his for the taking, body, heart and soul. Heat flooded every pore, advertising her compliance with any demand he chose to make. And he knew all of it, just from that kiss.

Sweeping her up into his arms, he took the steps three at a time and strode into the cabin, kicking the door shut behind him. Inside, the shadows were thicker, more concealing, the window merely a paler square of dusk.

He lowered her to the floor, sliding her slowly the full length of him until her feet made contact with the wooden boards. He traced the outline of her throat with gentle, callused fingertips, then followed their path with his mouth. He tugged remorselessly at the strings holding up her dress.

And she was terrified. Terrified that she'd make a fool of herself, that she'd disappoint him. Terrified that he'd stop. She felt the smooth cotton slip away, exposing her flesh in the dim light. She was hovering on the brink of the unknown and didn't know how to tell him.

She saw the shadow of him fling away his shirt. Heard the rasp of a zip, the soft thud of denim hitting the floor. Before she had time to be afraid of anything more, she felt the smooth, hard planes of him shift against her, and a deep and sensuous blackness blunted the edges of her timidity.

He was very sure how to please her. The sheet covering the cot lay as cool against her spine as a summer dawn, but his kisses possessed her with a fire that had been smoldering for days, and he gauged her dimensions with hands that knew precisely how to soothe the pebbles of apprehension prickling over her skin.

She had not guessed that the delicate triangle of flesh overlying her hipbones was a minefield of sensation, or that the hollow of her throat housed a thousand tiny nerves whose messages raced to the soles of her feet and back again. All she knew was that the length and breadth of him shielded her from the meager light and that his arms enfolded her in close protection. His every touch reinforced her certainty that what was happening between them was absolutely right.

She forgot that she was uninitiated in pleasing a man. Driven by a curiosity she'd never anticipated, she set about discovering him. She hadn't expected that, in places, his skin would feel as smooth and soft as hers, or that the muscles underlying it would tremble at her touch. In fact, she was so enchanted by the powerful conformation of him that she didn't notice how close he was to claiming all of her—until he touched her with an intimacy that nearly stopped her heart.

This time, the ocean was not there to intervene. She almost cried out a protest but, before the words had taken shape, he touched her again so beguilingly that she heard herself pleading for him please not to stop.

Little knots of tension twisted inside her, then came together in a writhing mass of desire that took control away from her and left her as helpless as the baby he'd earlier accused her of being.

Even she, novice that she was, knew she had achieved her intended goal and that they had reached a point of no return. She experienced an instant of sharp pain followed by a sudden hesitation on his part. Knowledge inherited from Eve had her closing about him, refusing him the option of second thoughts at this late stage.

Possessed by a different kind of love song, she clung to him, bemused by its driving rhythm. How could she have guessed that there would be such harmony? He was all strength and power and she perfectly designed to accommodate him, to match him heartbeat for heartbeat. If a small part of her cried out in disappointment when the cataclysmic explosion that shattered him spared her, she ignored it. She had everything she wanted, right there in her arms. For a few short moments, he was completely hers.

And then, too soon, she lost him.

She heard him fumbling with something on the small bedside table. The next moment a match flared and she saw his profile, stern and remote, as he touched the flame to a kerosene lamp. Its light danced shadows over the ceiling and chased the darkness into the far corners of the room.

He turned his head to look at her. The accusation in his stare unnerved her. "You were a virgin, weren't you?" he said, his voice flat with dismay.

There was no use denying it. One look at his face and she knew she had disappointed him, after all. "Yes."

He rolled away from her, swung his feet to the floor, and pulled on his clothes with a haste that added insult to injury. A chill took hold of her, a bone-deep, numbing cold that erased every trace of the warmth and passion they had shared.

She felt . . . oh, she felt lonely. Lonely and pathetic, and hopelessly inadequate. "Does it matter?" she asked timidly.

He groaned. "Yes, it bloody well matters!"

"Why?"

"Because I won't let you saddle me with that sort of responsibility."

Somehow, this wasn't what she'd envisaged. Where was that "after-the-loving" tenderness she'd expected? Should she have worn a sign that read "BEWARE: VIRGIN AT LARGE"? "I'm not asking you to assume responsibility, Jackson. It was my choice to come here tonight, and my choice to stay."

"Was it?" He glared at her. "Well, this is mine. I'm going down to the beach, and when I come back I want you gone. Out of my house and out of my life. Understand?"

The force with which he slammed the door shook the walls of the old cabin and snapped Laura free of her stunned inertia. *What in the world was so terrible about virginity*?

Scrambling into her clothes with even more haste than she'd shed them, she raced out of the cabin after him. He hadn't had the last word this time!

She found him sitting on a log, staring moodily out across the water. The rising moon cast ribbons of light over the waves and up the shore, bright enough for her to see the scowl on his face and the clenched muscles of his jaw. He looked formidably angry, but she was too irate herself to pay more than cursory attention.

"You've had your say and you'll see that I'm out of your house as ordered," she said in a low, furious voice, "but before I also remove myself from your life I have a few things to say to you. Quite why making love seemed such a wonderful idea somehow escapes me right now, but I'm adult enough to hold myself fully accountable for my actions no matter how much I might come to regret them later. At the very least, I expect you to behave with similar maturity instead of looking for a scapegoat to assuage your guilt—or whatever else it is that's put you in such a foul mood.

"Moreover——" she drew in a shoulder-heaving breath "—I always assumed, from everything I've read, that a man would feel honored to know he was the first—especially in this day and age. In light of that, I find your attitude insufferable."

He swore then, ugly words laced with a rage she couldn't begin to understand. "Don't play Lady Bountiful with me, Laura Mitchell. I'm not the sort of man who deals with other people's charity any better than he does their chastity."

Another thread of anger unraveled inside her. "I didn't force you to make love to me, and, unless I was sadly deceived, you weren't exactly reluctant to carry me off to bed."

"More fool me," he replied cuttingly.

"Well, I'm sorry if I disappointed you! Put it down to selective inexperience—if you're capable of appreciating such a thing."

To her dismay, she felt her chin quivering, and turned away, half blinded by the dazzle of moonlight on the tears suddenly trembling along her lashes. She'd rather die than let him see how much he'd hurt her. But before she'd taken more than a step or two he reached out one hand and grasped her not unkindly by the ankle.

"I didn't say I was disappointed," he muttered grudgingly.

"You didn't have to. It was self-evident."

He sighed, a man at odds with everything about life. "You're even more inexperienced than you think if you believe that, Laura."

He was touching her again, his fingers potently gentle. This was how she'd got herself into so much trouble with him to start with. "Take your hand off my leg," she said, without much conviction.

"I will," he replied, "if you'll do yourself a monumental favor and forget you ever met me."

She ought to agree. Every instinct at her disposal told her not to open the Pandora's box that she guessed he was close to offering. It would be best to cut her losses and run fast, now, while a few of her romantic ideals remained intact. But rational behavior was something that belonged to the time before she knew him, the time when her head had held uncontested sway over her heart. "What if I can't forget you? What if I don't want to?" she asked.

His hand slid away. "Then I shall have to make you," he said flatly.

She could sense the frustration boiling inside him, and knew she was pushing his very limited patience too far. But she knew, too, that no matter how hard he tried to persuade her otherwise she simply could not walk away from this night and forget it ever happened. It had changed everything for her. She was not the same Laura Mitchell who had woken up that morning, and she would never be that same Laura Mitchell again.

"It's much too late for you to do that, Jackson," she told him, "and the reason it's too late..." The enormity of what she was about to say hit her with disquieting impact. It was a bit like looking down on a rushing river from the top of a very high cliff, and knowing that jumping into the current and taking a chance on survival was the only option left open, because a raging fire stood at her back. She took a long, last breath and plunged. "The reason is that I love you."

He sprang to his feet. "Damn you," he raged. "Oh, damn you, Laura Mitchell! That's the second oldest trick in the world and I won't fall for it."

"You can't do anything about it," she cried.

One strong arm snaked out and reeled her in close to him. His eyes sparkled like very expensive, very dark sapphires, their fire sheathed in ice. "Oh, I think I can," he said softly. "I can tell you things about the man you claim to love that will send you fleeing back to the shelter of your well-bred world so fast that you won't even take the time to say goodbye."

"Nothing you have to say will change the way I feel," she insisted, and wondered why a scene that should have been laced with tenderness was rife with so much hostility and resentment.

"Oh?" His voice was silky with a menace that brought pin-pricks of fear racing over her skin. "Not even if I tell you that the man you're so certain you love served time in prison?"

"Prison?" she echoed stupidly. "What sort of prison?"

"The kind with steel bars and concrete walls, sweet face. The kind where they put men who've committed unspeakable crimes against society—murderers, thieves, and other illustrious types. The kind where uniformed guards carry rifles, and watch a man the whole time—when he's eating, when he's showering, when he's sleeping."

He inched closer so that his breath ruffled her eyelashes and she could see every line of his beautiful, sinister face limned in moonlight, feel every work-toughened contour of his beautiful male body next to hers. He took her chin in his hand, and tilted her mouth up to his. "Do you still want to kiss me now, Laura? Do you still want an ex-con touching your pretty little body?"

## CHAPTER NINE

LAURA shook her head. "I don't believe you. You're just saying this to get rid of me. You're making it all up, every word. I know you, I——"

"Do you?" Jackson's fingers manacled her wrist with impersonal, inflexible strength. "Tell me, Laura, exactly *what* do you really know about me?"

That I drown every time I look in your sea blue eyes, she wanted to say; that there's a magic in the air when you're near me that I've never felt before. Whether or not it makes sense, I recognized you the first moment I saw you. We belong together, and I want to grow old with you because you make me believe in happy endings.

But she could say none of those things because he would laugh and tell her she was a fool, so she searched for more tangible reasons.

"You're kind," she said, futilely trying to wrench herself free, "and you're gentle under all that iron self-control. You rescued Charlie, you danced with Honey Bee, who likes you and isn't a person easily deceived. You taught me to snorkel, helped me when I hurt my foot, and... oh, how do I know the sun will rise tomorrow, or that spring will follow winter? I just know, that's all."

They were rambling, feeble reasons perhaps, but how could she marshal an intelligent response when he was looking at her so strangely? "Jackson, don't make me keep this up. It isn't funny any more and you're hurting my wrists. Please let me go."

"You're free," he said, releasing her and spreading his fingers wide to demonstrate the truth of his statement, "and it's your own fault if you got hurt. You shouldn't have struggled like that. It's one of the first things they teach you when you get sent up, Laura: to go along with the system because the only person you'll hurt by fighting it is yourself."

He dusted off his hands and let them hang loosely at his sides. "Now, let's see, where were we? Oh, yes, you were counting my virtues. You weren't getting very far, were you?"

"It's not surprising, considering you're as close-mouthed as a clam, but that doesn't negate how I feel. Oh, I admit, in the beginning I thought it was just hormones gone crazy that drew me to you."

"It was," he assured her gravely, "and we both know better than to place much faith in them."

"But it didn't stop there, Jackson." Braving his displeasure, she stepped close to him again to run a hand up his chest and along the powerful curve of his shoulder. "I realized almost immediately that it was more than mere physical attraction, that you weren't just some mindless drop-out addicted to meditation and love beads. I recognized signs of culture that couldn't be disguised even though you were often rude and hostile. I thought I could never like you, but you became my friend anyway, someone I learned to respect for his intelligence and integrity, someone I learned to trust. You try to hide behind all that camouflage, Jackson, but if you're honest with yourself you'll admit that, at bottom, we're soul mates."

He said nothing, apparently content to wait as though, if he were patient enough, she'd finally wind down like a tiresome clock that wouldn't stop chiming. She found his silence far more unnerving than his earlier tirade, and let her hand fall away.

"I tried not to let this happen, Jackson. I told myself you were the wrong man at the wrong time and that, if I let myself fall in love with you, you'd break my heart." She sighed, a terrible desolation stealing over her. "And it's beginning to look as if that's the only part I managed to get right."

"No," he countered inexorably. "Filling in the blanks with a lot of romantic nonsense that won't stand the light of day doesn't add up to love, Laura. You admit I've been secretive and in the same breath claim to respect my intelligence. Don't insult it now by expecting me to believe you never questioned why I chose this sort of life——" he waved a hand expansively, taking in the sweep of the cove, the cliff, the ocean "—unmotivated by ambition, cut off from society, uninterested in money and all the other things by which success is measured."

He was frightening her, forcing her to confront questions she'd turned away from in the past because their answers led to disturbing conclusions. Oh, practicality was a loathsome thing, just like a friend who always gave the right advice then, when a person fell flat on her face, added insult to injury by saying "I told you so"! It had nothing at all to do with love.

"A lot of people have grown tired of the rat race," she protested.

"Perhaps—but how many of them do you count among your friends, Laura?"

She wasn't about to fall into that trap. "None," she admitted, "but then again, none of the socially or professionally ambitious men you obviously despise has appealed to me enough to make me fall in love with him. Perhaps if they had you wouldn't have ended up with a virgin in your bed tonight and we wouldn't be having this insane conversation now."

Couldn't she see this was killing him, that he couldn't bear it? He had always found her fine-boned elegance lovely, her demure curves alluring. Even now, in the midst of the destruction he'd brought about, he could take pleasure in the sight of her body; but her face... he could not look at her face!

He could not look at those clear, guileless eyes and watch them fill with bewildered pain without wanting to wipe away the hurt. He could not look at that soft, sweet mouth without wanting to brand it with his kiss. And he did not have, had never had, the right.

She deserved a whole man, someone able to give her everything she so desperately wanted to find in him. But he had known too much corruption, endured too much betrayal and humiliation, to be able to fit the mold. His soul was too vengeful, his heart too full of rage, to know love. And he did not know how to change that.

He turned away, the ache and futility of desire taking second place to the relentless pain buried inside that he'd carried for so long. However much he wanted her, he could not have her. And this was the real punishment, the ultimate price: to know that the freedom he'd craved throughout the last four years was meaningless without her. He had been released from one hell only to find himself the lifelong prisoner of another.

She reached up to cradle his cheek, appalled at the wretchedness in his gaze. "I know why you're playing this silly game, Jackson. You're trying to trick me into believing you're not good enough for me because you don't wear a thousand-dollar suit to work, or drive a Lamborghini. But don't you know that it's the man you are inside that matters?"

This time, he caught her hand and very deliberately removed it. "It's the man I am inside that convinced the courts to lock me up," he told her. "It's time you grew up and stopped believing in fairy tales, Laura. I'm not a hero in disguise."

Unnerved by his vehemence, her heart fluttered alarmingly and her fear slid closer to panic. "But I thought..."

What? That because she'd kissed him she *had* been able to turn him into a prince, just as Rose had accused? Had she really made a complete fool of herself over a pair of broad shoulders and a winning smile?

Oh, surely not! She'd been telling him the truth when she'd said it was more than his striking good looks that had stolen her heart. It was his sense of strength that relied not on power over other men but on inner fortitude. This was a man who would emerge proud and undefeated from the worst life had to hurl at him. He possessed the stamina and grace of a true thoroughbred.

"You're my kind of hero," she whispered.

He stood arrow-straight and calm, like a fallen angel who knew he would never again be admitted to paradise. And she stood on the other side, the wrong side. "No, I'm not," he said. "Stop being fooled by what you want to believe and understand what I'm saying. I served time in Stilwell Penitentiary. They let me out last March."

It couldn't be. She'd always known he was different from other men, but not because of something like this. "No!" she pleaded.

"Yes." His eyes were dark as midnight pools, his voice heavy with the conviction of absolute truth. "So, you see, we really aren't well suited at all. You're a woman of principle, Laura, full of an innocence that I doubt I ever possessed. You deserve the best—and I am flawed in ways you can't begin to comprehend. I cannot give you either what you want or what you deserve."

She felt crushed, shattered. Laura Mitchell of the high-and-mighty morals and superior good sense had fallen into bed with an ex-convict. Worse, she'd given him her heart, she'd trusted him. Trusted a man who'd been confined behind bars because it wasn't safe to let him loose on society!

As though moved by a glimmer of compassion for the devastation he'd wrought, Jackson took her hands and gently pressed them together as though he was giving her a final blessing. "Forget about me. Go back to your city, your art gallery, your full and happy life."

"It won't be full and happy without you," she quavered, making a last-ditch effort to hang on to a dream that was fading fast.

"It will if you let it."

"How does a person forget love, Jackson?"

He took a step away from her, the first of many that she knew would put miles and years between them if he had his way. "It isn't love, and you'll realize that much faster if you dwell on other things."

"We've shared some happy times. Remember——"

"Forget them and remember the down side: I'm an ex-convict. When happier memories try to sneak in, drive them out with that."

He was giving her an escape route, a reason to shrug off these last weeks. A reason to dismiss the message her heart was sending, and to listen to the sort of logic that had always ruled her life until she met him. She ought to be relieved—and couldn't be.

But if she was drowning in unhappiness and doubt, Jackson stood absolutely firm. "I do not want you," he said gently.

Because he neither raged nor snarled, she made one last effort to put the broken pieces of her dreams together again. "Would you," she whimpered, hating the pathetic, pleading note that had crept into her voice, "if you found you could fit into my sort of life despite everything that's happened to you?"

"I don't want to fit in," he stated with growing anger, and proceeded to destroy the last of her illusions. "I despise everything your sort of society stands for—its laws, its hypocrisy, its whole stinking system!"

She couldn't have been this mistaken. "No!" she cried. "I won't believe that!"

"Why not? Because it offends your sensibilities to think you fell into bed with a man who scorns the polite and proper scruples governing your polite and proper little life? Because people would pity you if they found out what you'd done?"

"They'd never have to find out——"

"No?" He sneered. "Don't kid yourself, sweet face. Sooner or later, it would all come out, and what would you do then? Feel compelled to justify me to your friends? Explain to Honey Bee or your mother that you haven't really thrown in your lot with a criminal, that I'm fully rehabilitated and safe to be around?"

"Why not, if it's the truth?"

"I'll tell you why not: because prison changes a man for the worse and he's never the same again afterward. Even if he were willing and able to forget his past, society isn't. The stigma of prison sticks to him whether he deserves it or not."

"But surely people could be made to understand——?"

"*You* don't understand, Laura," Jackson said harshly. "I won't hide behind your skirts, I won't be pitied, and I won't be patronized. So take your love and stick it!" He threw up both hands in frustration. "Hell, how much plainer can I make it? *I don't want you. Go away and leave me alone.*"

A red tide of passion welled up inside her then, composed of hurt and betrayal and hopelessness. It swept through Laura with blistering energy and erupted in a rage that had her rushing forward and slapping at him with wild, haphazard blows that landed without aim or regard for the damage they might inflict.

He stood there unflinchingly until her brief fury was spent. Then, "I gather I've convinced you," was all he said.

She leaned against him and let exhaustion and despair wash over her. Whatever she'd hoped for, whatever she'd believed, she'd been mistaken. He was a million dreams removed from the kind of man she'd wanted him to be.

"You've convinced me," she agreed dully.

The pity of it was, it had taken her so long to accept what he'd tried from the first to tell her. She'd seen the guarded look in his eyes, sensed the hostility, and had chosen to interpret them to suit her own misguided notions of romance, deluding herself into believing that she had love enough for two. She'd begged and she'd pleaded, and all she had to show for it was tattered pride and a heart so bruised and hurting that she might as well have invited him to drive a stake through it. And to think she'd had the nerve to criticize Rose for *her* unfortunate liaisons!

A sigh erupted, swollen with pain, and she'd already turned away, wanting nothing but to retreat from the scene of her humiliation with a modicum of dignity, when he spoke again.

"You haven't asked me why they locked me up," he said.

What did it matter? Murder, theft—they all came down to the same in the end. He'd stolen her soul, killed her spirit. She couldn't stand any of it, not what she'd let him do to her, nor what she'd done to herself. "No" she replied, her heartbeat thready with anguish. "I once thought I wanted to know everything about you, but I was wrong."

"And I was right," he said, his voice hoarse with what she might once have supposed was regret. "I knew from the first that you were a woman cast in the comfort of the conventional. A pearls-and-little-black-dress sort of woman. I should never for a moment have allowed myself to believe otherwise."

He turned her around and pointed her back toward the bluff. "Go back to where you belong, Laura, and find a socially correct man who deserves you."

He made it sound like an insult, as though the sort of man she needed would wear a tie to make love. And, to be fair, wouldn't she have been half inclined to agree, back at the start of the summer? Hadn't she told herself more than once that he really wasn't her type, that they came from two different worlds?

She had no business criticizing him. He'd done his best to discourage her, but she'd persisted in pursuing him with no more shame or finesse than a teenager obsessed with chasing down a movie-star idol. Unfortunately, she'd compounded the error by slipping into a fantasy of summer romance spiced with the thrill of sheer sexual magnetism, and been fool enough to believe it might be love. She ought to thank him for setting her straight. She ought to be relieved to discover he wasn't perfect and that she had every reason in the world to walk away from him.

She *was* relieved! *She was*!

So why was it so hard to leave? Her feet dragged as though trapped in quicksand, and she couldn't focus for the tears that filmed her eyes and robbed her of one last look by which to remember him. All she saw, when she half turned before beginning the climb up to the house, was the outline of him haloed in the dusk against the backdrop of the sea. All she heard over the painful lurching of her heart was Charlie's bark, and she remembered Jackson's reply, the day she'd asked him how he could bear ever to let the little seal go.

"He's got a right to his freedom, and it goes against everything I believe in to keep him in captivity one single day longer than necessary," he'd said with a passion she only now began to understand. "A man has to have a very good reason to do that to another living creature."

By the next morning, she looked a little bit like a pig with her eyes tiny and red-rimmed from crying. Honey Bee must have noticed, but when Laura muttered about having to get back to the city as soon as possible, because of a hitch in the upcoming exhibition, her great-grandmother acquiesced with her usual tact and said only that she hoped things wouldn't turn out as badly as Laura feared.

When she walked into the gallery the day after that, however, her partner, Archie, was less diplomatic. "You look like hell," he greeted her, his connoisseur's eye roaming over her face critically, as if he'd been presented with a bad reproduction on inferior canvas. "Was it something you ate, or someone you met?"

"Neither," she replied, refusing to get drawn into a conversation that could only bring back painful reminders of her gullibility. "I think I'm allergic to the sun. And I was worried about the amount of work still to be done here before the Fragonard exhibit opens."

He poured her a cup of evil-smelling coffee. "Bless you, my child! I don't believe you for a minute, but there is a mountain of stuff needing attention and I just don't seem able to get to the bottom of the pile before something else gets heaped on top. The infant howls from dusk to dawn, and neither Molly nor I have had a decent night's sleep in weeks."

"How is the baby?" Laura seized on the topic of the Hearsts' new son with gratitude. She wasn't sure how long she could keep up a facade of normality, so anything that would divert Archie's attention was preferable to his making her the focus of his scrutiny.

"He looks like something Michelangelo might have painted in the Sistine Chapel—chubby and angelic—until he starts screaming. Then he gets all scarlet in the face and reminds me of my mother-in-law."

Oh, she'd made the right decision in coming back here where she belonged, Laura thought, choking back a weak giggle. Throughout the endless hours that had passed since she'd last seen Jackson, she'd been afraid she'd never laugh again.

But then Archie threw an arm around her, gave her a squeeze and said, "You know, kiddo, if you ever need someone to talk to, Uncle Archie's a good listener. If there's someone out there who needs setting straight on anything, I'm your man." And at that she promptly burst into tears.

"I think I must be having an early mid-life crisis," she wailed, mopping her face with a wad of tissues. "I'm sorry. I know men hate women who get all weepy for no good reason."

"I'm used to it," Archie replied, stroking her hair. "Molly was just the same when she first got pregnant. Tears all the time, and they didn't stop until the morning sickness took over." He handed her a fresh supply of tissues. "Not that I'm implying *you're* pregnant, you understand."

Well, of course not! Laura Mitchell wasn't the type to take such irresponsible chances. Everyone knew that.

There was just one tiny flaw in the argument: Laura Mitchell was no longer a virgin. Was it possible...?

For the next two weeks, she put in twelve- and fourteen-hour days, preparing the gallery for the show. She met with dealers, prospective buyers, caterers. She ordered champagne, canapés, flowers. She uncrated canvases and custom-made frames. She kept busier than she'd have believed was humanly possible, because there were a thousand details requiring attention which left no time for Jackson Connery to creep into her thoughts, let alone the preposterous idea that she might be pregnant.

But at night, when she fell into brief, exhausted sleep, he slipped past her defenses in dreams as vivid as if time had run backward and it were high summer again. She heard his deep, beautiful voice accompanied by the low murmur of the surf, felt his hands bringing her to life, saw his eyes, bluer than forget-me-nots, laughing down at her. And awoke to a gray and lonely dawn.

Busy as she was, the days were as barren as a wasteland without him. He was gone as completely from her life as if he'd never existed outside her imagination, and she had nothing but heartache by which to remember him. Unless...

"It isn't possible," she told herself. "Women don't get pregnant the first time they make love. The odds are completely against such an occurrence."

But it's not unheard of, the obstinate, self-righteous voice of practicality nagged. And what will you do if, in fact, you are? What will you tell people? How will you face Honey Bee, or Rose?

Two weeks became three. She added dates on the calendar, allowing for a margin of error. She watched the cool September nights turn the first leaves outside the gallery windows to gold, and suspicion inched closer to certainty.

Meanwhile, Archie watched her. "You've got bags under your eyes, kiddo," he announced bluntly one morning. "Either buy some concealer or else stop staying out so late at night."

Good advice—except that she felt too wrung out to accept social invitations these days, and made the exhibition her excuse because she was too proud to admit she was pining for a man who didn't want her. She began sleeping poorly; she lost her appetite.

"If that's your idea of lunch," Archie declared on another occasion, inspecting her small carton of lemon yoghurt, "it's no wonder you've gone from slim to scrawny."

Don't flaunt your skinny endowments at me, Jackson had said. Everything always came back to Jackson and the probability of a baby with his eyes and his corn-silk hair. A boy? A girl?

An ex-convict's child, virtuous conscience pointed out implacably. If you can't dredge up shame, at least show regret and a little apprehension. Remember what they say about the sins of the father? Who knows what heinous crimes the man committed?

The old, foolish Laura, who thought she had all the answers and knew exactly what she wanted from life, might have agreed. But she'd disappeared some time between sunrise and sunset one fine summer day. The new Laura, who wasn't nearly as confident, listened to her heart, which told her that Jackson Connery was not a wicked person. No man who'd shown such kindness to an old lady, or such compassion for an injured animal, was capable of violence or evil.

He'd told her to be sensible, to face the facts and not try to glamourize them with a lot of romantic nonsense, but he might as well have saved his breath, because what it all came down to in the end was that it didn't matter to her that he'd been in jail, nor did it matter why. Despite all the reasons he'd given her for not doing so, she loved him, and there was no doubt in her mind that she would love his baby.

Would *he*, if he knew?

The question haunted her for days before she finally admitted to herself that there was only one way to resolve it. Maybe he'd turn her away, refuse to acknowledge any responsibility for the outcome of their brief affair. It was a chance she was willing to take. But one thing was clear: she had to go back and tell him. Not to trap him—no one would hold Jackson Connery against his will ever again; that much she knew for sure—but because he had the right to know that he had fathered a child.

And maybe the knowledge would draw on that deep well of tenderness that she knew he possessed, and bring a sweetness to his life that she thought must have been lacking for a very long time.

## CHAPTER TEN

LAURA chartered a float plane to Carter's Cove the following Friday afternoon. Honey Bee was delighted to see her, and openly appalled at how she looked.

"Only for the weekend?" she admonished, when Laura explained that it was quite literally a flying visit. "My love, if you value your health, you'll take more time than that."

"I can't possibly," Laura said. "The exhibition opens at the end of the month and as it is we're going to be hard-pressed to have everything ready on time."

"Then why don't you hire extra help?"

Because that would leave her with too much time to dwell on her personal woes, but Laura knew she couldn't say that without causing Honey Bee anxiety.

"At this late stage, a newcomer would only add complications," she explained and attempted to steer the conversation away from herself. "Are you still planning to come to town for the opening, Grandmother?"

Honey Bee looked up from pouring hot chocolate into delicate Austrian mocha cups. "Oh, I wouldn't dream of missing it," she replied with untoward energy. "I expect it to be a memorable evening."

Dressed warmly in a green mohair cape and matching suede pants, Laura set out the next morning to visit Jackson. A brisk westerly hurled breakers toward the shore and sent great puffs of cloud skimming across the sky. No doubt it all made a magnificent sight, but she was in no mood to appreciate it. She was an emotional mess, caught squarely between nervous anticipation at facing him with news that, at the very least, would come as a shock, and sheer terror at how he might react to finding her on his doorstep again.

The part of her that still believed in happy endings fantasized that impending fatherhood would bring about miracles; making a good life for his child would be more important to him than nursing a grudge against society.

Then the practical streak that she despised predicted that he'd be more distant than ever. The anger she'd always sensed in him, which was as much a part of him as the complexity of bone and muscle that made up the whole, would stoke itself to fresh heights suspecting she'd pulled another of the oldest tricks in the book to try to chain him to her.

He hadn't wanted the responsibility of her love, or her virginity. Was it really likely he'd feel differently toward a child?

As it turned out, all her anxiety was for nothing. The cabin, when she reached it, wore a desolate, abandoned air. Approaching it slowly at first from the beach path, she found herself almost running up the front steps as her arrival went unchallenged.

She knew without knocking that there was no one there to answer. Already a spider had spun its web over one corner of the doorway. Fir cones blown down in the last storm lay scattered on the porch. The dirt bike and the tarpaulin that covered it were gone. There was nothing of Jackson left about the place—nothing except a sliver of pink soap in a chipped saucer.

Stooping, she picked it up and breathed in its dying scent. Just fleetingly, time took another backward leap, evoking him with stark and perfect clarity. She saw again the chiseled purity of his freshly shaved jaw, the sultry blue of his eyes. Could almost feel his hand in the small of her back and almost taste the clean, beguiling flavor of his kiss. Even the wind conspired, soughing through the firs with uncanny melody. You made me love you, Jackson, it seemed to whisper.

Then the moment passed and she blinked, astonished to find the tears rolling down her face. In all the times she had envisioned the scene of her return not once had she imagined that he would not play a part in it. She had prepared for his displeasure, his scorn, his rejection, but never his disappearance. And the worst of it was, she hadn't a clue where to start looking for him. By now, he could be anywhere, Mexico, Tibet, Antarctica—he wouldn't care, as long as he was free to roam unshackled by responsibility to another.

What had happened to Charlie? she wondered, scrubbing at the tears that drizzled down her face like endless winter rain, leaving her sodden with despair. Had the little seal woken up one morning to find himself alone again? Or had Jackson taught him to survive in the wild before he'd abandoned him?

She pulled the cape more snugly around her and took a last look at the scene of her summer folly. It was time to go. The wind had picked up chilling strength in the last half hour and there was nothing to be accomplished here, after all. She might just as well reconcile herself to living with her unanswered questions and dealing with her situation the best way she knew how.

* * *

Laura returned to the city on Monday morning, and the following Wednesday went to see an obstetrician.

"Well," the doctor said, at the conclusion of his examination, "if it relieves your mind at all, Miss Mitchell, you're not pregnant."

It was not what she wanted to hear. "But I must be," she insisted. "I have all the symptoms."

"No," he replied, quite firmly, "you show all the symptoms of a young woman under stress who's neglected to take care of herself. Your blood is low, you're undernourished and, although I'm no psychiatrist, I'd venture to suggest you're deeply unhappy at this time. But you most certainly are not pregnant."

She was so distressed that she hardly remembered leaving his office and was surprised to find herself out on the street, with traffic roaring past and people jostling to get around her.

He was wrong. He had to be wrong. A baby was all she had left of Jackson.

But the doctor was right on all counts. Before the week was out, her body corroborated his diagnosis, and the intensity of her grief overwhelmed her. Jackson had gone from her life without leaving any legacy of himself, and she had to reconcile herself to living with a love that paid no heed at all to sense or logic, and that persisted despite her every attempt to shrug it off.

It didn't help to tell herself that it was perhaps all for the best; that Jackson Connery wasn't a man to be manipulated, not by a woman or anything else. He was boldly and invincibly unique and cared not a tinker's damn if his unorthodox attitudes offended more conventionally minded people.

Yet she couldn't help but wonder, would things have ended differently if, when he'd first told her he was an ex-convict, she'd said, "I don't care. I love you anyway"? Would he have believed her enough perhaps to look more fearlessly into his own heart?

She'd never know. More miserable than she'd ever been before, she drove herself even harder each working day, determined that the art show would be a success regardless of the fact that her personal life was a shambles.

She tried to forget Jackson, she really did. But the memories persisted in filtering past all the minor crises with which she busied herself each day. As for the nights... dear Lord, they seemed endless. She grew hollow-eyed from lack of sleep and paler than a snowdrop in January. And so alone that she didn't know how she'd go on.

"Kiddo," Archie protested, two days before the show opened, "you look like death warmed over. Do us both a favor and don't wear black on Friday evening, okay? We don't want people to think they've come to a wake."

He had a point. "Think you can manage on your own if I take the afternoon off?" she asked him on the Friday. "I thought I'd shop around for something to wear tonight, and then get my hair done."

"You'd leave me to cope alone at the eleventh hour like this?" Archie teased, sweeping his fingers through his own hair until it stood up in hysterical spikes. "What if the caterers let us down? What if the roof starts to leak? Where shall I find you? What shall I do?"

"There's enough champagne on ice to drown in," she said. "Crack a bottle and relax. I'll be back in plenty of time to fix any last-minute problems."

"Laura?" He caught her just as she reached the door. "Forget the gallery and its problems for the next few hours and treat yourself to the whole works—a facial and manicure and whatever else the salon has to offer. Not because you need the help, but because you deserve a little pampering." He gave her a hug. "Don't think I haven't noticed how hard you've been driving yourself the last few weeks."

"Maybe I will," she agreed. "It might relax me."

It turned out no such way, however, because while she was captive on the beautician's couch, with cucumber slices on her eyes and half an inch of egg whites and avocado drying on her face, her mother walked in.

"Emilio said you were here, darling. It's coming to something when the only place I can run my daughter to ground is in the beauty parlor."

"I can't talk," Laura muttered through stiff lips.

"Well, I can," Rose assured her brightly. "I received your invitation to the exhibition, which is why I'm here now, of course. I wouldn't want you to feel ashamed of me in front of all your important clients."

"Don't be absurd, Rose."

She heard the click of a lighter, smelt the expensive brand of Russian tobacco that her mother favored. "You're always so righteous, Laura. Always so sure of yourself. Do you think I don't see the contempt in your eyes when you look at me? Or don't you care that it hurts me to know my only child despises me?"

"Mother, this is hardly the time or the place——!"

"It never is, for us." Rose inhaled, then expelled a stream of smoke overlaid with the scent of perfume, and went on in a voice that seemed on the verge of cracking, "Having no one is a wicked thing. It frightens me more than almost anything else, I think—the thought that I could die in my apartment and not be missed for days. That's why I sometimes wish we knew each other better, but of course you're far too busy being successful."

She gave a brittle laugh quite unlike her usual merry chime. "I can imagine what you're thinking: that we haven't been close since your father's death when you were a little girl, and that I've left it a bit late to start worrying about mother-daughter bonding. No doubt you're right as usual, but sometimes I wish the young could be a little more tolerant of their less-than-perfect parents."

Rose inhaled again, a quiveringly pathetic breath. "I'm not like you, Laura. I don't have your self-sufficiency. I never did have. I've always leaned on other people's strength, and I didn't think an eight-year-old child could give me the kind of support I needed when your father died. So, I looked elsewhere, and you turned to your beloved Honey Bee when you should have been able to turn to your mother. I don't blame you, darling. I just wish it weren't too late for us to get to know each other well enough to be...well, to be friends, I suppose, if nothing else."

"Mother——" Laura could hardly speak for the pain in her chest. She felt as if she'd been slashed open and every nerve laid bare. How easy it was to judge other people's shortcomings and be blind to one's own! She didn't feel self-sufficient at all. She felt more like a little girl who badly needed her mother's comfort and support.

"It's all right—I know you think I'm a silly, emotional woman afraid of growing old alone." When she laughed, Rose didn't sound like Tinkerbell any more. She sounded old and sad and rather brave. "Emilio's probably ready to start my hair by now, so I won't embarrass you further. I don't know what prompted this cathartic little outburst. I really just stopped in to wish you good luck tonight, darling, in case I don't get the chance to speak to you later. I'm sure everything will be quite wonderful, as usual."

Laura heard Rose's high heels tap on the marble-tiled floor and the louvred door of the cubicle swish open. "Mother, please don't go."

There was a moment's silence, then, "My heavens, Laura, you're crying. Don't do that, darling—you'll ruin your facial. And don't worry, I won't embarrass you tonight by showing up with someone unsuitable. In fact, I plan to come alone."

"You won't be alone. I'll be there, and so will Honey Bee."

"Well, of course. Honey Bee is always there for you."

Laura swallowed and tried again. She'd spent a lifetime protecting herself from what she'd perceived to be her mother's indifference, and never once suspected her loneliness. It wasn't easy, now, to be unafraid of honesty. She held out a hand blindly and wished she could wipe out all the years of estrangement. "But you're my mother," she said in a watery voice, "and I don't think I can make it through tonight without you."

High heels clicked rapidly over the tiles again. Laura felt her mother's elegant hands clasp hers. "Oh, darling," Rose whispered, obviously aghast, "whatever is the matter?"

From the minute the doors opened at seven o'clock that evening, a succession of chauffeured cars and limousines rolled into the plaza and stopped under the canopied awning outside the gallery. From their vantage point on the center landing of the branched staircase that led from the mezzanine level down to the main salon, Laura stood beside Archie and looked over the assembled guests.

It could have been a scene lifted from a Renoir painting. Except for the track lighting strategically angled to display the artwork to best advantage, the area below was illuminated by the soft gleam of chandeliers. The women shimmered beside their more soberly clad menfolk. However gaudy male attire had become in recent years, the classic black dinner jacket with pleat-fronted white shirt was very much in vogue again.

"We're a hit, kiddo!" Archie exulted, straightening his bow tie for the umpteenth time. "We've got Press coverage from Los Angeles, Chicago and points east, as well as all the local papers, and just look at the jewels and designer outfits down there."

From behind the cover of her fluted champagne glass, Laura whispered discreetly, "Stop fidgeting, Archie. You're on TV."

"Right." Archie beamed expansively and, as a news-coverage crew zoomed in for a close-up, offered his best profile. "Everything looks great—the flowers, the food, all that polished silver. And bringing in the pianist complete with baby grand was an inspiration." He angled an appraising glance her way. "So are you, come to that. Is that the new dress?"

"Yes. Like it?"

He grinned. "Do bears live in the woods? What amazes me is how you managed to get your hair fixed up like that and still find time to go shopping."

"I almost didn't," she admitted. She and Rose had had a manicure together then gone to the indoor tea garden in one of the large hotels where they'd spent more than two hours trying to make up for almost twenty lost years. Laura wasn't quite sure which had amazed her more—that she'd confided to her mother things she hadn't revealed to another living soul, not even Honey Bee, or that Rose had received the news of her daughter's involvement with Jackson Connery with relative equanimity.

"I'm sorry he hurt you, darling," Rose had murmured regretfully, "but at the same time I'm rather grateful to him, shady past notwithstanding. If it weren't for him, you and I probably wouldn't be sitting here together, now. As for love at first sight—heavens, darling, don't be too ready to dismiss it as nonsense. It does happen. It's just that most people have such fixed ideas about the proper way for things to occur that they refuse to listen to what their hearts tell them."

"Is that what happened to you, Mother?"

Rose had sighed and nodded. "With your father, yes. He wasn't interested in being successful and making money, you know, and I thought happiness couldn't be had without either, so we more or less went our separate ways when you were very little. By the time I finally realized that he was the best man in the world for me, he'd left on the climbing expedition to the Himalayas, where he died." She shrugged graceful shoulders. "And I've been looking ever since for someone to measure up to him."

The wistful note in her mother's voice, and her look of naked gratitude at being included in the shopping trip to find an outfit for tonight's affair, had made Laura ashamed of her aloofness in the past and bitterly sorry for all the wasted years when she and her mother could have been close. Jackson had been right when he'd accused her of taking people too much at face value, as she was learning to her cost.

Rose came up the stairs just then, all smiles and airy kisses that didn't quite connect. It didn't matter; her hug was warm and genuine. "Darling," she said, "I knew the dress would outshine everything else on display, and it does. It brings out the color in those marvelous Carter eyes you inherited and which I've always envied. You look elegant, Laura. Beautiful, in fact."

It *was* a lovely dress, a deep, rich mallard green with hundreds of matching hand-sewn beads and a handkerchief hem, and Laura knew it suited her. But beautiful? She shrugged dismissively. "I wouldn't go quite that far, Mother. I'm a pretty plain individual underneath."

"Rubbish! You've got that air of breeding about you that never grows old or passé—good bones and skin, and proportions that designers dream about when they come up with their most elegant creations. Twirl around, darling, and see how the beads glitter. Aren't they the most adorable little confections?"

"Adorable little confections' were not something Laura would ever rhapsodize over, but that didn't mean she wasn't warmed by her mother's approval. The dress was a triumph made all the more memorable by the pendant emeralds Honey Bee had bequeathed to her on her twenty-first birthday. They swung from her ears now, regally overpowering the beadwork on her gown.

"Isn't that your great-grandmother who just arrived?" Archie asked, inclining his head toward the double doors where specially hired security guards stood sentinel. "There—see her?"

Laura followed his gaze but it wasn't Honey Bee, resplendent in black velvet and diamonds, who caught her eye. It was the crush of guests coming through the door behind her great-grandmother, and one man in particular—who stopped her breath and left her heart laboring. It might have been a trick of the light, or just that she looked for him everywhere she went but, just for a second, Laura thought she saw Jackson. And then the crowd shifted and the image was gone.

"Hey, kiddo!" Archie's concern sifted through the layers of shock weaving foggily around her. "Are you going to keel over on me?"

"I hope not." Her voice trembled with a mixture of dread and disappointment. "But, just to be on the safe side, will you excuse me for a moment?"

She flung Archie and her mother an apologetic glance and fled into her private office located to the left of the landing. A one-way window on its north wall gave her a bird's-eye view of the entire lower floor. Separating the slats of the blind covering the glass, she pressed her eye to the opening. Honey Bee stood before one of the exhibits, deep in conversation with a man who bore no resemblance whatsoever to Jackson. Tall and good-looking he might be, but he was also close to sixty and what little hair he had left was solidly gray.

She must have had too much to drink! Crushed by disappointment, Laura plunked down her glass so hard, it was a wonder it didn't shatter. As it was, the remaining two-thirds of its contents splashed over the polished surface of her desk.

Oh, damn! Just when she thought she was taking control of her life again, some vague Jackson Connery look-alike reached past her defenses and touched her heart with killing regret for what might have been. Plucking tissues from a box at her elbow, she mopped at the puddle and swallowed the incipient tears. She would not cry over spilt champagne or spilt milk!

Behind her, the door opened and Archie's head appeared. "Sorry to break in on your solitude, Laura," he said, "but if you're feeling up to it, I really think we ought to circulate. The early arrivals will be leaving soon and we don't want to miss out on potential sales."

"Of course." She tucked a spare tissue into her evening bag. "Is my mother still waiting for me?"

"No, she went to speak to your great-grandmother, but there's a man down there who's come looking for some specific piece of art and he refuses to deal with anyone but you. Says you've had previous dealings with him, but I don't recall seeing him here before tonight."

"What's his name?"

"Johnson...no, that's not it...it's a double-barreled name..." Archie fished distractedly in his pockets and riffled through about twenty business cards. "One of these is his, but I'm damned if I—

Ah, here it is—Jackson Connery, no first name or initial."

The hum of success interwoven with the piano music of Paganini floated up the stairs. Just to prove to herself that she was quite sane and not drifting in a living daydream in which she first thought she saw him, then thought she heard Archie speak his name, Laura smiled at the unlikelihood of Jackson's ever deigning to be seen at a gathering like this.

"You must be mistaken," she said, wondering how Archie could possibly hear her voice over the faltering hammer of her heart. "There's only one Jackson Connery that I know of and he's the last man in the world I'd expect to see here."

"Then prepare to be surprised," Archie told her, and held out his arm. "Not only is he here, my dear, he seems quite anxious to speak with you. Let's not keep him waiting."

She was conscious of heads turning as she and Archie made their way down the curving staircase. Dozens of eyes watched them—brown, gray, hazel. And one pair so startlingly blue that it was as if a breath of summer had gate-crashed the début of society's fashionable winter season.

Her heart did more than falter then. It braked to a shocked standstill. There was no dismissing him as a figment of her imagination this time. Tamed and trimmed to executive perfection his hair might be, but nothing could dull its radiance any more than prison had dimmed Jackson's pride.

Seemingly aware that his particular magnetism exerted a force field greater than the sum total of everyone else's, the crowd parted and opened a path that led directly to where he waited.

"Ah!" Archie cleared his throat and, as though on cue, the ranks of guests flowed around them again. "I believe you two already know each other so I won't waste time on introductions, but if I can be of any help...?"

Jackson dismissed him with the merest tilt of his head and Archie obligingly melted into the crowd before Laura could beg him to stay while she made a dash for the door. Beyond the tumult of her thoughts, a tiny core of sanity photographed the confident grace of Jackson's long-legged stance, the supremely elegant fit of his dinner jacket across the width of his shoulders, and focused at last on his unsmiling mouth.

At that, her fortitude crumbled and her throat closed in a spasm of longing. He was here, her beloved rebel, close enough to touch yet rendered doubly unfamiliar in this unlikely setting.

Her mind scrambled to restore order out of chaos. She opened her mouth without being sure just what she might say, and prayed only that she wouldn't grovel at his feet and make an utter fool of herself. "How did you know where to find me?" she heard herself ask.

His voice, laced with the richness of molasses, stroked down her spine. "I made it my business to find out," he said, and took a step closer.

On every side, the low cadence of conversation picked up volume, swirling around but leaving them untouched. She had no ears for anyone but him, no eyes for any face but his. She was filled with the scent of him, the heady masculine blend of starched linen and sweet summer breezes underscored by the teasing hint of clean, warm skin. Sure that her eyes revealed the longing she couldn't repress, she looked down, veiling herself from his gaze with her lashes.

His shoes gleamed blackly. If she did disgrace herself by collapsing on the floor, some aberrant portion of her mind remarked, she'd probably be able to see her face reflected in their shining leather. She risked another glance at him. "Why have you come?" she asked, her voice a tiny, painful bleating that struggled past the constriction in her throat.

"Because I hate loose ends, and far too many exist between you and me." He indicated the guests still milling around. "When can you get out of here?"

In all the times she'd imagined their meeting again, it had never unfolded like this, among a crowd of elegantly dressed connoisseurs bent on spending small fortunes on original artwork. It reminded her of why she was there to begin with, and she seized on the reason with gratitude. "Not for quite some time, I'm afraid. I'm working."

He snagged a glass of champagne from a passing waiter's tray and raised it in a gesture more threatening than salutational. "Oh, it will have to be much sooner than that. I'm not a patient man, Laura."

# CHAPTER ELEVEN

NEITHER patient nor reasonable! Jackson's glare elicited an answering flame of anger within Laura. Was the whole world expected to march to the rhythm of this one man's drum? Or was it just that he was obsessed with keeping other people off-balance all the time? Because, when it came to loose ends, there were a few bothering her.

For a start, he was the man who'd sneered in contempt for her sort of life. That being so, what was he now doing, rubbing shoulders with society's upper crust? Furthermore, how had he made his way past the security guards without an invitation, and where had he dug up his finery? She didn't claim to be an expert on men's clothing, but she knew a custom-tailored dinner suit when she saw one.

"And I'm not disposed to jeopardize the success of my gallery's most important event just because you choose to show up—uninvited, I might add—and snap your fingers for me to come running. It's been nearly two months, Jackson, so why the big rush all of a sudden?"

"I missed you." Jackson's lashes swept down then swooped up again. His gaze smoldered, blatantly making love to her in front of a roomful of people.

Oh, right! she wanted to retort. You can say things like that, just the same way those sultry eyes of yours can send messages that are barely decent, as long as enough people are around to prevent your having to back up either statement with proof or action!

"Have you?" she remarked witheringly. "Well, I've spent the last miserable month or more trying to regain a toehold on the sort of contentment I once took for granted, and I'm not sure I want you coming back——"

"And what sort of contentment is that?" he interrupted silkily.

"The sort that comes from plying a respectable profession and generally leading a life of blameless unadventure."

"I don't think there's any such word," he said, his mouth curling into the ghost of a smile.

"Oh, yes, there is!" she shot back bitterly. "And I'm living proof of it—an atrophying virgin with the imagination of a gnat, who's perfectly happy being a 'pearls-and-little-black-dress sort of woman,' remember?"

He reached out and tested her earlobe with his fingertip, causing her earring to sway like a pendulum. "These aren't pearls," he murmured. "They're emeralds as full of fire as your eyes, and suit you much better."

Even so slight a touch aroused in her the swift tug of desire. Rage at her body's perfidy scalded her neck and raced to her cheeks. "Don't maul me," she threatened breathlessly.

His brows arched in astonishment. "I'm guilty of many sins where you're concerned, Laura, but mauling you isn't among them. There were times when I certainly wanted to shake you, disgust you, enrage you—anything, as long as I drove you away—because I thought you were too fragile to withstand the shock of associating with a man with my past. And far too ready to accommodate a man of my hunger. I was afraid I'd break you, one way or another."

"Too ready to accommodate a man of your hunger?" Outraged, she pounced on the description. "Good grief, why don't you just come right out and call me a slut?"

"Lower your voice, sweet face," he suggested, pressing a finger to her lips and casting a wry glance around the room. "You're attracting all sorts of shocked attention. And not for a moment did I mean to imply that you were—ahem—a lady of dubious character."

The rotten rogue was laughing, as though she'd said something hilarious. She wrenched her mouth free of his touch. "You almost did break me," she said stonily, "but I can assure you I won't let it happen again."

"No, you won't," he agreed, his eyes roaming her face, feature by feature, "because you've got a clarity of vision that, until recently, I lacked. You're an intelligent, successful woman who knows where she's headed and is sure of what it takes to make her happy."

And he was a devil of the worst kind because his horns were hidden under that handsome facade. She hardened her heart. "Is that why you're here now, Jackson? Because you respect my professional expertise and want a little guidance in purchasing some fine art?"

"You know damned well it isn't," he growled. "I'm here because you and I are an unfinished picture, and I'm not going away until the last brush stroke is in place. Those are my terms, so you might as well accept them."

Everything had always been on his terms—that was the whole trouble. And, even knowing that, her heart was crying out for him, whether or not he was prepared to negotiate a fair and equitable settlement. It was time to put a little starch in her own bargaining powers. "Then make an appointment to see me next week when I'm not busy with other things," she informed him.

"Like hell," he told her. "I already told you—I'm not leaving until you and I come to an understanding, sweet face."

Heavens, he was more arrogant than ever. It must have something to do with the clothes. "Then stand here and grow roots," she informed him, "but resign yourself to my not keeping you company. There are other people who'd like to talk to me and I've kept them waiting quite long enough. And don't call me sweet face!"

She swept away, the beads on her dress chattering applause, and wove a determined path through the crowd before he had the chance to detain her. Almost at once, the other guests converged on her—the rich, the discerning and the influential coming together to toast the gallery's success.

"An impressive showing, my dear..."

"Such a pleasure—we're captivated by the little watercolour hanging on the wall at the foot of the stairs..."

"...an extra catalog, perhaps? We'd love to send one to our daughter. She and her husband are avid collectors, too."

"...cheap at half the price. Crate it up and send it out to the house..."

For the next two hours, the pace didn't slacken. Like the well-bred creature she prided herself on being, Laura managed all the correct responses and half succeeded in pushing Jackson to the back of her mind—that was, until the McIntyres came along. Charles McIntyre was a prominent businessman who'd worked hard to achieve his success, but Margery, his wife, was a classic example of *nouveau riche* vulgarity at its worst.

"A wonderful evening," Charles began. "We'd like to come back when it's not quite so crowded." He paused and inclined his head to some point just behind her. "By the way, Laura, I'm so glad to see you included Jackson Connery on the guest list."

Laura's self-possession slipped a notch. "Well... naturally," she replied, slewing her gaze over her shoulder. To her surprise, she found Jackson the center of interest of a group of well-known personalities of whom the mayor was but one, and, as far as Laura could determine, he seemed well-known by all of them.

Charles McIntyre straightened and tugged on the lapels of his dinner jacket. "I'd heard rumors that he was back and taking up the company reins again. High time, too."

Despite a small fortune spent on acquiring the social graces befitting the wife of a high-powered business mogul, Margery McIntyre had a voice like a fishwife's. It overrode the general buzz of conversation now and brought heads swiveling toward her. "But Charles, isn't he the man who got sent to prison over some dreadful stock-market scam?"

"Unfortunately, yes, Margery, and a damned shame it was too. Don't you agree, Laura?"

"Definitely," Laura murmured, aware of Jackson's gaze homing in on her with the intensity of a laser beam. Don't justify me to your friends, it reminded her, because I won't be pitied and I won't be patronised. Nevertheless, she couldn't let Margery McIntyre's comment pass unchallenged. "And since it's all in the past now I see no purpose in dragging the whole business up again."

"But my dear!" Margery objected shrilly. "He's hardly the sort of person you'd want to see your daughter bring home for dinner, is he—if you know what I mean?"

"No," Laura replied levelly. "I'm not sure I do, Mrs. McIntyre."

The other woman tittered nervously. "Well, let me put it this way. I wouldn't want him involved in any of *my* affairs, financial or otherwise. He's kept the wrong kind of company and learned too many bad habits over the last few years."

"Margery, that's enough!" Charles McIntyre's face was ruddy with embarrassment and, far from wanting to prolong the evening, he was clearly anxious to make as speedy an exit as dignity would allow. "Jackson Connery is a damned fine man and a damned fine broker. I'd trust him to handle my investments any day. The pity of it is that an old, respected family firm like Kilbourne and Connery had its reputation dragged through the dirt because its senior partner couldn't keep his fingers out of the till, and the fact that he let his nephew take the rap is a bloody crime. If Jackson Connery has the guts to bounce back from that sort of low blow then more power to him, because it's going to take someone with his sort of drive and integrity to rebuild that company and put it back on top again."

He took Laura's hand and shook it warmly. "My dear, we will be back. I'm interested in two or three paintings but we really are pressed for time right now. Come, Margery."

Laura watched them go with mixed feelings. She wished Charles McIntyre had said enough to satisfy the curiosity that she couldn't suppress, but it was a relief to see the back of his wife. Diplomacy was obviously not one of Mrs. McIntyre's strong points, and Laura had cringed inside at the woman's blunt insensitivity.

Jackson had seemingly been right when he'd said the stigma of prison stuck to a man. He'd been right when he'd said that she was the kind who'd feel compelled to defend him and offer explanations. In fact, he'd been right about so many things that Laura couldn't imagine him ever being wrong—all of which brought her back full circle to the question of why he'd shown up here tonight hinting that theirs was an unfinished picture after all, despite his previous certainty that he didn't want anything to do with her and her misplaced love.

Archie, his face flushed with the excitement of success, appeared at her side. "Hey, kiddo, the James-Margetsons have to leave shortly and they're interested in Exhibit Forty-seven. Since you're the one who knows its history, they'd like to have a word with you before they go."

"Of course." Laura tucked her hand beneath Archie's elbow and, aware that Jackson's gaze shadowed her every step, walked to the front entrance where the James-Margetsons waited.

Jackson watched the beaded dress sway around her as she glided away, and was unable to drag his eyes from the sight even though Tom Robinson, CEO of one of the major investment companies on the Pacific coast, was trying to interest him in a merger. Who'd have thought the day would come when a woman's hips and blazing green eyes would distract Jackson Connery from business?

But distract him they did. Her hips, like the rest of her, were gorgeous. And the eyes were blazing every time they looked his way—blazing with anger.

He wasn't surprised. Not for a moment had he expected that the mere fact of his showing up tonight would cause her to fling herself into his arms and say all was forgiven. In fact, he'd have been disappointed if she had. His woman wasn't the sort to let a man trample all over her, then thank him for the abuse. No doubt about it, he had a few fences to mend before the night was over, but if anyone had learned to take his punishment the hard way, he had, and he knew now that he was a survivor.

"What do you say, Jack?"

"That she's worth every second of aggravation she's given me."

"Huh?" Tom Robinson's well-fed jowls quivered with confusion. "Say what, Jack?"

Why was her partner hanging on to her elbow that way? If she couldn't stand on her own two legs unaided, Archie Hearst wasn't the man she should be turning to for support. "Some other time, Tom, okay? I've got business cooking tonight."

"I hoped I had, too," Tom replied dolefully. "Can we get together for lunch next week, perhaps?"

Jackson nodded. "Sure, but it's only fair to warn you I'm not looking for outside partners. I plan to keep the company in the family."

"You don't have any family," Tom pointed out.

Jackson feasted his eyes on Laura's narrow waist, on her elegant ankles peeking out from beneath that peculiar hem. Did she know it wasn't cut straight? "Give me time, buddy," he murmured. "Give me time."

As so often happened when a large group was gathered together, the sight of one or two people preparing to leave seemed to prompt the remainder to do likewise and, after her discussion with her clients, Laura was faced with saying good-night to a crowd.

Throughout, Jackson maintained his surveillance of her, managing at the same time to exchange a round of back-slapping bonhomie with a couple of land developers and a broker or two. The degree of frank geniality he exhibited to them, and which had been so markedly absent in his past association with her, made her blood boil all over again.

Like a well-behaved wind-up doll, however, she nodded and smiled at the departing guests until her face ached. She couldn't wait for them all to be gone so she could make her own escape. Beside her, Archie fielded questions with an adroitness she envied. She only hoped there'd be no late arrivals. If she had to shake another hand, she was afraid her palm would stick like glue.

No more than a dozen people remained when Rose came to her. "Darling, is everything all right?" She inclined her head to where Jackson now stood flanked by Wallis Roscoe, one of the city's most respected bankers, and his well-corseted wife. "I mean to say, we could always have him thrown out, if that's what you want. You haven't looked exactly ecstatic to see him here, you know."

Honey Bee materialized from behind a pillar and tapped her on the arm. "Don't interfere, Rose. Things have never been better."

"I don't know how much you know about that man," Rose objected, "but I happen to think he has some explaining to do and, from the look on Laura's face, I'd say he's not been very forthcoming."

"I trust him implicitly," Honey Bee replied blithely. "That's why I gave him my money to invest."

"I'm not talking about Mr. Roscoe, Grandmother!"

"Neither am I," Honey Bee said.

Rose blanched. "Grandmother, you can't possibly mean you've put the family fortune at risk by handing it over to Jackson Connery? Extenuating circumstances notwithstanding, the man's past bears some investigation."

"We all have skeletons in our closets, my dear Rose. Some are just more colorful than others, that's all. Rest assured that I'm fully acquainted with Jackson's unhappy past. As for the money, it's mine to do with as I please and I'll paper the walls with it if I so choose." Honey Bee smiled in Jackson's direction and received a warm grin in return. "As it happens, though, I've put it to much better use. Good night, Laura."

Something more than Laura had first realized was going on here, and her great-grandmother, the person she probably trusted most in the world, was in on it. "You knew he was going to be here tonight! You invited him, didn't you, Honey Bee?"

Honey Bee nodded, an unashamedly sly twinkle in her eye. "The time was ripe for a little helpful interference, my love."

Rose quivered with indignation. "My good heavens, Grandmother, I do believe you're losing your senses!"

"Fiddlesticks!" Honey Bee reached up and pressed a kiss to Laura's cheek. "Call me tomorrow, dear child. I'm in my usual suite at the Hyatt and I'll be waiting to hear from you."

They weren't properly out of the doors before Jackson made his move. As though he'd deliberately waited to catch Laura at her most vulnerable moment, he came up behind, slipped her jacket over her shoulders, and settled cool fingers against the flushed skin of her neck.

"Time to say good-night to everyone, Laura," he said.

She shrugged him off. "For you, certainly, but I have a few more social obligations to attend to."

A steeliness crept into his voice, one she remembered only too well. "No, you haven't."

"Not everyone has left," she pointed out icily. "There are still at least five other couples——"

"I can count as well as you, Laura, just as I know as well as you that your partner is admirably capable of taking care of the few people remaining."

"I'm the hostess! It's my——"

He smiled, a purely barbaric, entirely bewitching and beautiful smile. "I just ran out of patience, sweet face," he murmured and, without batting an eye, hoisted her over his shoulder as if she were a well-dressed sack of potatoes and marched out of the door with her.

A car, long, sleek and powerful, came gliding out of the night and whispered to a halt under the canopied entrance to the gallery. "That's not my car," Laura snapped breathlessly, as Jackson set her back on her feet.

"It's mine. I use it for business," he replied, opening the back door before the driver had time to hop out and do the job himself. "Get in."

He didn't quite shove her but, if her heels had been an eighth of an inch higher, she'd probably have toppled onto the leather seat nose first as the finale to her undignified exit from the gallery. "If you're not careful," she raged, "you'll find yourself charged with kidnapping—and it won't be fabricated evidence that puts you away this time!"

Ignoring her, Jackson climbed in beside her and tapped on the glass separating the driver from his passengers. The car pulled smoothly out of the plaza and turned south on the main thoroughfare.

Appalled at what she'd said, Laura huddled in her corner of the back seat, her unwarranted threat still singeing the air. Jackson maintained a dignified silence. Leaning forward, he slid open a panel to reveal a stereo system and a well-stocked bar, poured brandy into thin balloon glasses, and handed one to her. Then he settled himself at the other end of the wide seat, as far away from her as he could possibly get.

In the fleeting glare from passing streetlights she saw that his expression was solemn. Deeply ashamed, she averted her gaze. She hadn't thought herself capable of such stark cruelty toward anyone, let alone a man she'd once professed to love.

"I'm sorry, Jackson," she said in a small voice. "That was an unforgivable thing to say."

He swirled brandy around his snifter and stared at it consideringly. "When you had every reason to hate me, you told me you loved me," he finally said. "Why, now that you must know I am not entirely without merit, are you so determined to dislike me?"

"Because I'm afraid of you. I don't understand you."

"I am what you see," he said softly. "A man only lately come to his senses."

But that was too glib a dismissal of the pain she'd endured because of him. "How can I believe you?" She gestured at the luxury around them. "Look at all this, at you. What's happened to that man on the beach who sent me away because he had nothing but contempt for the trappings that were part of my way of life?"

"Is that what this is all about? The fact that I'm not a penniless vagabond?"

"No," she retorted, her anger flaring up again. "It's about you letting me believe that's all you were. You rejected me—made me feel shallow and foolish—because I cared about convention and respectability, and you weren't about to adapt to that sort of life. Then you show up at the gallery tonight, and I find you fit in very well. You're very much at ease. You even know half the guests." She snatched an irate breath. "And it occurs to me that our whole association has been one long joke—on me."

"It's odd that you should see yourself as the victim of a joke," he said mildly, "because that's more or less the way I felt when I found I'd been duped by someone I thought I could trust. It hurts, doesn't it, when someone you care about treats you shabbily? It takes rather a long time to forgive."

"Yes, it does, but two wrongs never made a right."

"Perhaps not, but even saints make mistakes sometimes. Have you never been wrong, Laura?"

She thought about her mother, and closed her eyes on a spasm of shame. "Yes."

"Then can you not try to forgive me for having taken so long to come to my senses, or at least understand that, until I did, there was no good purpose to be served in my reappearing in your well-ordered life?"

"You make me feel smug and complacent," she complained, "when all I ever wanted was to understand. Yet how could I, when you refused to let me share anything about your life up to the day I met you?"

"I wasn't ready," he told her.

"And now you are."

"Yes," he said.

She laughed bitterly. "And you really think that your sudden reappearance is all it will take to erase the last two months, Jackson? Good grief, I might have lost my business if I hadn't had Archie here to pick up the slack while I suffered a minor breakdown over a man who'd disappeared off the face of the earth and taken my heart with him."

"I never expected you'd go back to the cabin looking for me," he said. "When Honey Bee told me you had, it was all I could do not to come to you then, before you found someone new. But there are times when being too soon is as bad as being too late, and I was still rebuilding my life. I had to take the chance that your feelings for me wouldn't change before I succeeded."

There was nothing to be gained by telling him the reason she'd gone back to find him. They had enough to sort out between them for now without muddying the issues with mistaken notions of pregnancy.

"Where were you, Jackson, during all those long, painful weeks when I was trying to recover from the foolishness of loving you?"

"Right here in town, Laura—and please tell me you don't mean it when you say loving me was foolish."

The deep, bemusing cadence of his voice had almost seduced her into forgiving him—until she realized what he'd admitted. She shot forward to the edge of the car seat.

"*Right here in town*? And you never once bothered to pick up the phone, or stop by the gallery?" To think she'd wondered and worried about where he might be and how he might be managing, and all the time he'd been living within a stone's throw—and doing so rather well if tonight's trappings were any indication. "Why didn't you, Jackson? Was it too much trouble? Too inconvenient to find a phone in such a well-populated place? Or were you perhaps too busy picking up the threads of a life that held no room in it for a 'pearls-and-little-black-dress' woman like me? Was I too dull for your new, sophisticated image?"

"Why did I ever open my big mouth and call you that?" he asked ruefully. "I can see I'm going to have the devil's own time living it down."

"Never mind feeling sorry for yourself," she retorted pithily. "What's the real truth here, Jackson Connery? Did you decide to rejoin the human race because you hoped to pick up with some old flame who'd been waiting patiently in the wings until you found yourself? Was that why you were so appalled at having made love to another woman who was an inconvenient virgin to boot?"

"Does the thought that I was make you jealous, sweet face?"

Until that moment, Laura had never been quite sure how a person actually gnashed her teeth. It was a purging discovery. "I could throttle you," she declared with utter sincerity.

He smiled his fallen-angel smile, and turned his summer blue eyes her way. "At least you're not indifferent to me, darling, even though, for all you really know, I'm nothing but an ex-con guilty of everything they accused me of."

"I might be mired in conventionality, Jackson Connery," she replied, "but I trust my instincts enough to know that you're incapable of real evil. I don't know why they locked you up, and—God help me—I decided weeks ago that I don't even care."

He reached across and took her hand, smoothing his fingers over her palm and up her wrist with telling effect. "I wasn't guilty of any crime, Laura, except possibly my own stupidity, which left me totally unprepared for the morning when I came into my office and found myself under arrest. That day a nightmare began that took years to unravel."

He acted full of calm acceptance but, even so, vestiges of old hurt ran through his voice. They softened Laura enough to ask, "Why did it take so long for you to be exonerated?"

He rested his head against the car's plush leather upholstery. "I come from a long line of stockbrokers,

Laura. My grandfather on my mother's side started the family business, her younger brother and my father carried on with it, and eventually I joined. My parents were so thrilled when that happened that I'm glad they didn't live long enough to witness my fall from grace. When this mess all started, I'd just turned twenty-nine and earned my junior partner's stripes."

The air crackled with tension as the memories resurfaced. "My uncle, who taught me just about everything I know about the market, set me up to be the patsy for his own dishonesty. Quite simply, investigators found laundered certificates which they traced to my account, and when they went through my office they found more—in the desk, the filing cabinet, the bookcase—hell, even in my briefcase. And I couldn't explain how I'd come by any of them. I'd never seen them before."

"Why would your uncle do a thing like that?" Laura was aghast. Whatever her weaknesses, Rose would never have stooped to cheating and lying, and certainly not against her own daughter.

Jackson shook his head. "Men get greedy, Laura—even those who have more money than they can comfortably spend. In my uncle's case, he invested heavily in the market and made some bad trades. He saw a lifetime's capital slip through his fingers in a few short months and he grew desperate. He started buying hot securities, selling them, then depositing the cash in nominee accounts with U.S. addresses, because they're hard to trace. He might have got away with it indefinitely if one of the insurance companies hadn't identified some of the securities as being stolen. Of course, my uncle knew at once when our company came under investigation because he was primed for the possibility of such an event. And he took adequate precautions against having suspicion point to him."

"How did you eventually prove yourself the victim instead of the perpetrator?" Laura asked.

"The old man decided to try the same stunt again last year, to make up what he didn't recoup the first time around. Since I was safely behind bars, there was no way I could be blamed, and that initiated a new full-blown investigation that led straight to my uncle's door."

"So he's behind bars now?"

Jackson's laugh was a bittersweet blend of affection and disillusionment. "Actually, he had a heart attack and died—but not before I was released from prison and had the chance to visit him one last time. And do you know what the old rogue said? That he set me up because he figured I was young and tough enough to start over again after I'd served my sentence, but that, at his age—he was in his mid-sixties—he didn't have the luxury of time on his side. Not a word of regret or shame, just pure outrage that fate had caught up with him and cheated *him* in the end!"

Laura had no reason to disbelieve a word. The entire account had an authentic ring of truth to it, even without the evidence of Charles McIntyre's corroborating facts. And, at heart, she wanted nothing more than to put the past away and set her sights on a future that looked much rosier than it had yesterday at this same time. But one thing still troubled her.

"If everything was this simple and straightforward, why couldn't you have told the whole story at the beginning? Why did you pass yourself off as a beachcomber with barely two cents to rub together? You ought to know better than most how hurtful such deception is."

He was silent for a moment, then, "Yes," he said. "I do. And I'm not very proud of the way I treated you."

She withdrew her fingers from his. "Was clarifying all this why you came to the gallery tonight, Jackson? Were these explanations the loose ends you referred to that you wanted to see neatly tied up?"

"Yes," he said.

"Why?" Her voice faltered and grew thin. "So that you could go forward with your life with a clear conscience, knowing you hadn't left a trail of deceit and misrepresentation behind you?"

"Yes," he said again, making no attempt to recapture her hand.

So that was it. He wanted absolution, and she'd thought perhaps he wanted love.

She turned away from him and stared blindly out of the window. They'd left the downtown area long ago and were traveling along a tree-lined crescent of grand old houses tucked away behind yew and holly hedges. A minute later, the driver slowed to negotiate the car through a pair of gates and up a driveway bordered with rhododendrons and azaleas.

The car purred to a halt under a gray stone *porte cochère*. "Why have you brought me here?" she asked Jackson as the chauffeur came around to open the door. As far as she was concerned, the sooner this whole painful evening was over, the better.

"Because there's one last loose end remaining to be tied off before I can close the book on my past and make plans for my future. And because I counted on the fact that you're fair enough to give me the rest of this evening in which to redeem myself, even though I haven't always been fair with you." He dropped his voice to a beguiling murmur as the chauffeur extended a hand to help her out of the car. "Was I wrong?"

Emotion rippled through her, escaping on a long, trembling sigh. How easily he wormed his way around her! "Half an hour," she conceded.

The night was thick with the scent of evergreens and wet, freshly turned earth. From somewhere below the house, the swish of waves punctuated the honk of a foghorn farther out to sea.

"What is this place, Jackson?"

"The house where I grew up."

House? It was more like a mansion! And yet why should she be so surprised, when she'd felt from the start that he possessed a civilized grace thoroughly at odds with the backwoods image he worked so hard to preserve?

The interior of the house was quite breathtaking. Magnificent rugs covered the planked oak floors, brass and silver gleamed, crystal shimmered. It was a warm and lovely home and in different circumstances Laura would have been enchanted by it if only because, in many ways, it reminded her of the happy times she'd spent with Honey Bee in Carter's Cove. Jackson's house possessed that same air of having been loved and cared for by successive generations of one family.

"Let me take your jacket," Jackson said.

"No." She pulled it more snugly around her, as though by doing so she could ward off evil spirits. "I already told you, I won't be staying very long. You've answered my questions."

All but one—and that she didn't want to ask for fear of what he might answer. He'd talked about everything except how he felt about her, and the omission sat like lead inside her.

He opened a door on the right. "Will you at least come in here? It's my study, not a torture chamber."

She supposed it couldn't hurt. "Very well."

He crossed to the fireplace and struck a match to the kindling laid ready. A painting on the wall above the mantelpiece showed a man, arrestingly handsome, with piercing blue eyes and a mouth so full of sensuous promise that it must have shocked the women of his era. He gazed out at the world as if he owned it.

Jackson at sixty would look just the same, Laura thought. "Is that your father's picture hanging on the wall?" she asked, as he straightened up and came to stand beside her.

"My grandfather." A rumble of laughter escaped him. "And from your tone I gather you'd like to see me hanging next to him, preferably by the neck?"

"Don't presume to read my mind, Jackson," she reprimanded him, "and I won't presume to understand yours."

He turned to face her. "In other words, cut out the small talk and let's get down to the last reason I brought you here, right, Laura?"

## CHAPTER TWELVE

LAURA nodded. "Precisely."

"I don't suppose you'd agree to sit down?"

"No." She turned to the window and stared out at the night but all she saw was the reflection of the room at her back.

Jackson sighed faintly. "Very well. Since we said goodbye last summer, I've been busy."

"So I gather," she said.

"There were certain priorities I felt I had to take care of."

And she obviously hadn't been one of them!

"Reestablishing myself in the business world came first, of course, and——"

"Of course!"

"And restoring this house to its former glory," he continued steadily, "came next. It had stood empty for almost five years, with only a weekly visit from a caretaker to make sure the place didn't fall down. It looked pretty dismal when I came back, with half the furniture in storage and the rest covered in dust cloths and cobwebs."

"My goodness!" Laura exclaimed ironically. "I never would have guessed you were so house-proud, considering the place you were living in when we met."

Jackson watched her for a full minute or more, then let fly with a spate of language too colorful to pass for restraint, even if his voice was pitched low. Before she had a chance to fend him off, he'd covered the distance separating them and imprisoned her in his hold.

"Sometimes," he growled, "actions not only speak louder than words, they save a hell of a lot of time, too, and, since I suspect you're determined either to ignore or discount any explanation I try to offer, perhaps you'll believe this instead."

It was bad enough that he fastened his mouth on hers and stung her lips with a kiss whose sweetness she couldn't resist, but how much worse that the reserve she'd so carefully nurtured melted away faster than ice under a blazing tropical sun.

Do *not* kiss him back! her outraged pride insisted, but her mouth had a will all its own. She tried to push him away, and clung to him instead; tried to contain desire and felt a thousand bubbles of passion explode over her skin.

It ought not to be like this. She should have discovered that her imagination had created a myth that couldn't possibly measure up in the flesh. He should have been a little less tall, a little less handsome, and a whole lot less devastating than memory had made him. Instead, he was everything that—and more than—she remembered, and she knew with hopeless dismay that no other man would ever take his place.

She hadn't really expected otherwise. All she prayed for was the strength to withstand him because he wielded such a capacity to inflict hurt on her. It had taken her countless hours and endless weeks to fight the symptoms, only to discover in the space of a few hours that she was as susceptible as ever to the disease.

Dear Lord, she thought despairingly, as Jackson's kiss deepened and swept her into ever more dangerous waters, was she going to spend the rest of her life paying for the forbidden pleasure of one short summer?

"Stop it!" she gasped, tearing herself free.

Whatever else his failings, he was not one of those men who interpreted "no" to mean "yes." He released her and, returning to lean against the mantelpiece, stared down at the flames in the hearth, his eyes haunted. "Are you afraid of me?" he asked at last.

"Yes," she said quickly, before the pain in his expression made her recant a truth she couldn't afford to deny.

His voice sounded raw. "Why?"

"Because you hurt me very badly before."

He squeezed his eyes shut, the way a man did when he was in agony. "What will it take to make you trust me again, Laura?" he asked, on a strangled note.

"Oh, Jackson...!" Her voice was thick with tears suddenly. Of all the emotions he'd aroused in her, the one he'd most undermined was her trust. Did he think that simply asking her to renew it would be enough to repair the damage? Yet her love had survived the blow and, even now, the incessant tug of desire had her gravitating toward him and reaching up one hand to wipe away the misery that left him grim-faced and silent. "Why did you have to come back into my life now, just when I thought I was over you?"

"Because it's taken me this long to straighten myself out. I was an angry man when you first met me, Laura. Angry and bitter. I'd been betrayed by my uncle—the man who gave me my first pair of skis, who taught me to sail, and whom I'd looked up to and admired for as long as I could remember. My name, my reputation, had been dragged through a messy inquiry. I'd been charged with embezzling thousands—hundreds of thousands of dollars. And when I stood before a judge and proclaimed my innocence, certain that the truth would triumph, I was found guilty and sentenced to five years in prison. And the society in which I'd been brought up, and by whose rules I'd always played, turned its back on me."

"But your conviction was overturned," she reminded him. "That same society admitted its error."

"Yes," he agreed, and, even though the room was warm and she still had on her jacket, the chill in his voice seeped into her bones. "But by then it had taken two years of my life that I'll never get back. Can you understand the sort of rage that inspired in me, Laura?"

In a way, she could. She'd frittered away years distancing herself from her mother, but she knew the regret she felt didn't compare to the injustice of what he'd suffered. "Perhaps not," she said, "but what was to be gained by wasting more time feeding on that rage? Your innocence had been proved before the whole world and you were free to assume your rightful place in society and pick up where you left off."

His laugh was laced with mild exasperation. "My sweet and sheltered innocent, didn't I try once before to explain to you that it takes more than an official apology and a clean record to wipe away the taint of having been accused in the first place? I work with other people's money—their lifesavings, their security against an impoverished old age—and there's an old adage that says there's no smoke without fire. Would you place your trust in a man like me, when there are plenty of other capable brokers out there without a hint of scandal attached to their names?"

She'd trust him with her life, if only he'd give her reason to believe he wanted to be a part of it. "But that's so unfair!" she protested.

He stirred the flames in the hearth and added another log. "I know," he said. "And the unfairness ate at me until I had to get away before I killed someone. Prison teaches a man a different set of values, Laura. It makes him grateful for simple things, like watching the trees turn green in the spring, or having a choice of what he eats for dinner. 'Freedom' takes on a whole new meaning, and I wasn't about to be shackled by the restrictions of a life that used to be mine and which didn't seem to fit me any longer.

"So, I rejected the society that had once rejected me. I believed," he finished wryly, "that I was making an important statement. Kids did it all the time in the sixties, renouncing convention for long hair and love beads. It took you to make me realize I was a bit too old for such immature rebellion."

His image in the glass was all blurred, as if the rain were streaming down the windowpanes, and she heard the foghorn again, even though the night outside was clear. The moon hovered above the trees and pinpoints of starlight flecked the sky. They were her own tears brimming over that warped the reflection, just as his anger had distorted his perception of life. "So why have you come back now, Jackson?" she asked on a trembling note.

"Not because I want to make you cry," he said.

She swallowed to no effect. The tears clustered along her lashes. "Oh..." Her voice was drenched with the promise of raindrops waiting for the merest breath to shake them loose. "I've done a lot of crying lately."

He stepped a little nearer but didn't touch her. "Because of me?"

How little she'd taken into account his suffering, immersed as she'd been in her own pain. She felt the first tear spill and, with it, a tiny easing in her heart. "Because of me. Because I saw only what I wanted to see, even though you warned me to look past the obvious. And because I've been obtuse and unfair."

He touched her then, stopping the recriminations with a finger against her lips. "I hoped," he murmured, with incomparable tenderness, "that you were going to say because you love me the same way I love you."

They were words she'd longed to hear him speak, yet perversity had her scolding him. "Then why," she cried, "did you take so long to tell me?"

"I wanted to be good enough for you."

"You were always good enough," she said passionately.

"Thank you for saying that, my darling, even if you are wrong."

She turned his hand over and kissed his palm. "You were the one wronged," she whispered. "I know that now."

"But you were the one I punished." He backed to the armchair beside the fire and pulled her down onto his lap. "I was so busy hanging on to my anger that I wasn't about to let happiness or love soften it into forgiveness." He grimaced. "It's called making a career out of misery, I believe, and, if I do say so myself, I was pretty successful at it."

"What made you decide to change?"

He threaded his fingers through her hair, dislodging all the pins and mussing up the fancy styling. "I remembered a fellow inmate from prison—a doctor, a wonderful man who was convicted of manslaughter because he honoured a patient's wishes to die with dignity. Just before I was released, he told me, 'Don't be a martyr, Jackson. In the long run, everyone ends up getting hurt.' And I finally realized he was right. In driving you away, I'd ended up punishing both of us, and for the first time in a long time I was suddenly tired of harboring the grudge. But I knew that until I got the poison out of my system I couldn't move on with my life."

"Where does Honey Bee fit into all this?"

"She was one of the few people who'd always accepted me as I was and always treated me with respect. I felt she had a right to know the whole story, especially since my future plans included her beloved Laura, so I went to see her before I pulled up stakes in Carter's Cove and moved back to the city. I wasn't sure how much you'd told her and I wanted to be sure she knew that my intentions regarding you were entirely honorable. I'd hoped she wouldn't oppose me, but I hadn't expected she'd give me her blessing."

"Honey Bee understood us from the start."

"Yes, she did," she said, "and that was one reason I kept her informed of my progress in picking up the pieces where I'd left off. I wanted her to know her faith hadn't been misplaced——" He angled an oblique glance at her from under his absurdly long eyelashes. "And it gave me the chance to keep tabs on what you were doing."

"You spied on me!"

"In a manner of speaking, yes."

"You could have saved me weeks of misery." She tugged a handful of his hair, hard. "Why did you take so long?"

"Because I couldn't accept your love until I'd set my life back on track. You deserved better than a sour, embittered dropout living in an old fishing shack."

"I would have lived with you in a tent," she murmured, sliding her arms around his neck, "as long as I knew you loved me."

"I know," he said. "That was why I wanted to offer you more."

"Money isn't the most important thing, Jackson."

"But being the best you can be is. When a woman like you gives a man her heart, she deserves a whole person in return. And that's what I had to find, Laura—the parts of me that I'd lost. Now that I've recovered them, will you take them, for better or for worse?"

His kiss was an entreaty. At that moment, she would have walked barefoot to the North Pole if he'd asked her. "Yes," she said.

He shaped the words against her mouth with unbearable sweetness. "For richer, for poorer...?"

Her heart soared. "Yes," she said.

"Will you love me and forsake all others?"

"There aren't any others," she said. "There's never been anyone like you."

"And may I call you 'sweet face' sometimes, just for old times' sake, and because it's true?"

"Yes," she sighed. "Is there anything else?"

"No."

"Then may I ask you something?" She hated to cloud the moment, but there was one last thing bothering her.

He kissed her with prophetic intent and tampered with the handkerchief hem of her dress. The beads rustled with anticipation. "Anything."

"What happened to Charlie?"

He nuzzled her neck. "I brought him with me, of course."

"He's *here*?"

"Not in this very room, but he's around, probably down on the beach. I'm surprised you haven't heard him barking."

"I heard a foghorn..."

Jackson's kiss dissolved into laughter against her mouth. "It's a clear night, Laura, and that was no foghorn—that was Charlie."

She shook her head disbelievingly. "You actually brought him to town with you?"

"Mmm-hmm. Your friend at the aquarium was right. Charlie thinks I'm his mom. Lucky for us we'll be living next to the beach. When he's old enough to explore the wider world, he won't have far to travel. It's waiting on his doorstep." Jackson strung a row of kisses along her jaw to the corner of her mouth. "Any more questions?"

Happiness was bursting inside her like champagne bubbles, leaving her light-headed with bliss. How could she ever doubt a man who'd adopt an orphaned seal? "A request, maybe."

He trailed his mouth down the length of her neck and forgot to stop when he reached her throat. The straps holding up the mallard green gown obligingly slipped down her shoulders. "Name it," he said.

"Will you take me upstairs and make love to me?"

"Any time, sweet face," he murmured. "For the rest of my life, if you'll let me."